Apart from enjoying an enviable reputation
as one of the best writers on the science
fiction scene, Harry Harrison is a man of
wide interests and accomplishments.
A first-class short story writer, an
experienced editor and anthologist, a
translator (from Danish and Italian),
a trained cartoonist, he has also been a
commercial illustrator, hydraulic press
operator, truck driver and is, of course,
a first-rate novelist.

Two Tales and Eight Tomorrows

HARRY HARRISON

SPHERE BOOKS LIMITED
30/32 Gray's Inn Road, London WC1X 8JL

First published in Great Britain
by Victor Gollancz Ltd 1965
Copyright © Harry Harrison 1965
Published by Sphere Books 1976, reprinted 1977

To Robert P. Mills

Set in Monotype Plantin

Printed in Great Britain by
C. Nicholls & Company Ltd
The Philips Park Press, Manchester

CONTENTS

Somewhere above, hidden by the eternal clouds of Wesker's World, a thunder rumbled and grew. Trader John Garth stopped when he heard it, his boots sinking slowly into the muck, and cupped his good ear to catch the sound. It swelled and waned in the thick atmosphere, growing louder.

'That noise is the same as the noise of your sky-ship,' Itin said, with stolid Wesker logicality, slowly pulverizing the idea in his mind and turning over the bits one by one for closer examination. 'But your ship is still sitting where you landed it. It must be, even though we cannot see it, because you are the only one who can operate it. And even if anyone else could operate it we would have heard it rising into the sky. Since we did not, and if this sound is a sky-ship sound, then it must mean . . .'

'Yes, another ship,' Garth said, too absorbed in his own thoughts to wait for the laborious Weskerian chains of logic to clank their way through to the end. Of course it was another spacer, it had been only a matter of time before one appeared, and undoubtedly this one was homing on the S.S. radar reflector as he had done. His own ship would show up clearly on the newcomer's screen and they would probably set down as close to it as they could.

'You better go ahead, Itin,' he said. 'Use the water so you can get to the village quickly. Tell everyone to get back into the swamps, well clear of the hard ground. That ship is landing on instruments and anyone underneath at touchdown is going to be cooked.'

This immediate threat was clear enough to the little Wesker amphibian. Before Garth finished speaking Itin's ribbed ears had folded like a bat's wing and he slipped silently into the nearby canal. Garth squelched on through the mud, making as good time as he could over the clinging surface. He had just reached the fringes of the village clearing when the rumbling grew to a head-splitting roar and the spacer broke through the low-hanging layer of clouds above. Garth shielded his eyes from the down-reaching tongue of flame and examined the growing form of the grey-black ship with mixed feelings.

After almost a standard year on Wesker's World he had to fight down a longing for human companionship of any kind. While this buried fragment of herd-spirit chattered for the rest of the monkey tribe, his trader's mind was busily drawing a line under a column of figures and adding up the total. This could very well be another trader's ship, and if it were, his monopoly of the Wesker trade was at an end. Then again, this might not be a trader at all, which was the reason he stayed in the shelter of the giant fern and loosened his gun in its holster.

The ship baked dry a hundred square metres of mud, the roaring blast died, and the landing feet crunched down through the crackling crust. Metal creaked and settled into place while the cloud of smoke and steam slowly drifted lower in the humid air.

'Garth – you native-cheating extortionist – where are you?' the ship's speaker boomed. The lines of the spacer had looked only slightly familiar, but there was no mistaking the rasping tones of that voice. Garth wore a smile when he stepped out into the open and whistled shrilly through two fingers. A directional microphone ground out of its casing on the ship's fin and turned in his direction.

'What are you doing here, Singh?' he shouted towards the mike. 'Too crooked to find a planet of your own and have to come here to steal an honest trader's profits?'

'Honest!' the amplified voice roared. 'This from the man who has been in more jails than cathouses – and that a goodly number in itself, I do declare. Sorry, friend of my youth, but I cannot join you in exploiting this aboriginal pesthole. I am on course to a more fairly atmosphered world where a fortune is waiting to be made. I only stopped here since an opportunity presented to turn an honest credit by running a taxi service. I bring you friendship, the perfect companionship, a man in a different line of business who might help you in yours. I'd come out and say hello myself, except I would have to decon for biologicals. I'm cycling the passenger through the lock so I hope you won't mind helping with his luggage.'

8

At least there would be no other trader on the planet now, that worry was gone. But Garth still wondered what sort of passenger would be taking one-way passage to an uninhabited world. And what was behind that concealed hint of merriment in Singh's voice? He walked around to the far side of the spacer where the ramp had dropped, and looked up at the man in the cargo lock who was wrestling ineffectually with a large crate. The man turned towards him and Garth saw the clerical dog-collar and knew just what it was Singh had been chuckling about.

'What are you doing here?' Garth asked; in spite of his attempt at self control he snapped the words. If the man noticed this he ignored it, because he was still smiling and putting out his hand as he came down the ramp.

'Father Mark,' he said. 'Of the Missionary Society of Brothers. I'm very pleased to . . .'

'I said what are you doing here.' Garth's voice was under control now, quiet and cold. He knew what had to be done, and it must be done quickly or not at all.

'That should be obvious,' Father Mark said, his good nature still unruffled. 'Our missionary society has raised funds to send spiritual emissaries to alien worlds for the first time. I was lucky enough . . .'

'Take your luggage and get back into the ship. You're not wanted here and have no permission to land. You'll be a liability and there is no one on Wesker to take care of you. Get back into the ship.'

'I don't know who you are sir, or why you are lying to me,' the priest said. He was still calm but the smile was gone. 'But I have studied galactic law and the history of this planet very well. There are no diseases or beasts here that I should have any particular fear of. It is also an open planet, and until the Space Survey changes that status I have as much right to be here as you do.'

The man was of course right, but Garth couldn't let him know that. He had been bluffing, hoping the priest didn't know his rights. But he did. There was only one distasteful course left for him, and he had better do it while there was still time.

'Get back in that ship,' he shouted, not hiding his anger now. With a smooth motion his gun was out of the holster and the pitted black muzzle only inches from the priest's stomach. The man's face turned white, but he did not move.

'What the hell are you doing, Garth!' Singh's shocked voice grated from the speaker. 'The guy paid his fare and you have no rights at all to throw him off the planet.'

'I have this right,' Garth said, raising his gun and sighting between the priest's eyes. 'I give him thirty seconds to get back aboard the ship or I pull the trigger.'

'Well I think you are either off your head or playing a joke,' Singh's exasperated voice rasped down at them. 'If a joke, it is in bad taste, and either way you're not getting away with it. Two can play at that game, only I can play it better.'

There was the rumble of heavy bearings and the remote-controlled four-gun turret on the ship's side rotated and pointed at Garth. 'Now – down gun and give Father Mark a hand with the luggage,' the speaker commanded, a trace of humour back in the voice now. 'As much as I would like to help, Old Friend, I cannot. I feel it is time you had a chance to talk to the father; after all, I have had the opportunity of speaking with him all the way from Earth.'

Garth jammed the gun back into the holster with an acute feeling of loss. Father Mark stepped forward, the winning smile back now and a bible taken from a pocket of his robe, in his raised hand. 'My son,' he said.

'I'm not your son,' was all Garth could choke out as defeat welled up in him. His fist drew back as the anger rose, and the best he could do was open the fist so he struck only with the flat of his hand. Still the blow sent the priest crashing to the ground and fluttered the pages of the book splattering into the thick mud.

Itin and the other Weskers had watched everything with seemingly emotionless interest, and Garth made no attempt to answer their unspoken questions. He started towards his house, but turned back when he saw they were still unmoving.

'A new man has come,' he told them. 'He will need help with the things he has brought. If he doesn't have any place for them, you can put them in the big warehouse until he has a place of his own.'

He watched them waddle across the clearing towards the ship, then went inside and gained a certain satisfaction from slamming the door hard enough to crack one of the panes. There was an equal amount of painful pleasure in breaking out one of the remaining bottles of Irish whiskey that he had been saving for a special occasion. Well this was special enough, though not really what he had had in mind. The whiskey was good and burned away some of the bad taste in his mouth, but not all of it. If his tactics had worked, success would have justified everything. But he had failed and in addition to the pain of failure there was the acute feeling that he had made a horse's ass out of himself. Singh had blasted off without any good-byes. There was no telling what sense he had made of the whole matter, though he would surely carry some strange stories back to the traders' lodge. Well, that could be worried about the next time Garth signed in. Right now he had to go about setting things right with the missionary. Squinting out through the rain he saw the man struggling to erect a collapsible tent while the entire population of the village stood in ordered ranks and watched. Naturally none of them offered to help.

By the time the tent was up and the crates and boxes stowed inside it the rain had stopped. The level of fluid in the bottle was a good bit lower and Garth felt more like facing up to the unavoidable meeting. In truth, he was looking forward to talking to the man. This whole nasty business aside, after an entire solitary year any human companionship looked good. *Will you join me now for dinner. John Garth,* he wrote on the back of an old invoice. But maybe the guy was too frightened to come? Which was no way to start any kind of relationship. Rummaging under the bunk, he found a box that was big enough and put his pistol inside. Itin was of course waiting outside the door when he opened it, since this was his tour as Knowledge Collector. He handed him the note and box.

'Would you take these to the new man,' he said.

'Is the new man's name New Man?' Itin asked.

'No, it's not!' Garth snapped. 'His name is Mark. But I'm

only asking you to deliver this, not get involved in conversation.'

As always when he lost his temper, the literal minded Weskers won the round. 'You are not asking for conversation,' Itin said slowly, 'but Mark may ask for conversation. And others will ask me his name, if I do not know his na . . .' The voice cut off as Garth slammed the door. This didn't work in the long run either because next time he saw Itin – a day, a week, or even a month later – the monologue would be picked up on the very word it had ended and the thought rambled out to its last frayed end. Garth cursed under his breath and poured water over a pair of the tastier concentrates that he had left.

'Come in,' he said when there was a quiet knock on the door. The priest entered and held out the box with the gun.

'Thank you for the loan, Mr Garth, I appreciate the spirit that made you send it. I have no idea of what caused the unhappy affair when I landed, but I think it would be best forgotten if we are going to be on this planet together for any length of time.'

'Drink?' Garth asked, taking the box and pointing to the bottle on the table. He poured two glasses full and handed one to the priest. 'That's about what I had in mind, but I still owe you an explanation of what happened out there.' He scowled into his glass for a second, then raised it to the other man. 'It's a big universe and I guess we have to make out as best we can. Here's to Sanity.'

'God be with you,' Father Mark said, and raised his glass as well.

'Not with me or with this planet,' Garth said firmly. 'And that's the crux of the matter.' He half-drained the glass and sighed.

'Do you say that to shock me?' the priest asked with a smile. I assure you it doesn't.'

'Not intended to shock. I meant it quite literally. I suppose I'm what you would call an atheist, so revealed religion is no concern of mine. While these natives, simple and unlettered stone-age types that they are, have managed to come this far with no superstitions or traces of deism whatsoever. I had hoped that they might continue that way.'

'What are you saying?' the priest frowned. 'Do you mean they have no gods, no belief in the hereafter? They must die . . . ?'

'Die they do, and to dust returneth like the rest of the animals. They have thunder, trees and water without having thunder-gods, tree sprites, or water nymphs. They have no ugly little gods, taboos, or spells to hag-ride and limit their lives. They are the only primitive people I have ever encountered who are completely free of superstition and appear to be much happier and sane because of it. I just wanted to keep them that way.'

'You wanted to keep them from God – from salvation?' the priest's eyes widened and he recoiled slightly.

'No,' Garth said. 'I wanted to keep them from superstition until they knew more and could think about it realistically without being absorbed and perhaps destroyed by it.'

'You're being insulting to the Church, sir, to equate it with superstition . . .'

'Please,' Garth said, raising his head. 'No theological arguments. I don't think your society footed the bill for this trip just to attempt a conversion on me. Just accept the fact that my beliefs have been arrived at through careful thought over a period of years, and no amount of undergraduate metaphysics will change them. I'll promise not to try and convert you – if you will do the same for me.'

'Agreed, Mr Garth. As you have reminded me, my mission here is to save these souls, and that is what I must do. But why should my work disturb you so much that you try and keep me from landing? Even threaten me with your gun, and . . .' the priest broke off and looked into his glass.

'And even slug you?' Garth asked, suddenly frowning. 'There was no excuse for that, and I would like to say that I'm sorry. Plain bad manners and an even worse temper. Live alone long enough and you find yourself doing that kind of thing.' He brooded down at his big hands where they lay on the table, reading memories into the scars and callouses patterned there. 'Let's just call it frustration, for lack of a better word. In your business you must have had a lot of chance to peep into the darker places in men's minds and you should know a bit about motives and happiness. I have had too busy a life to ever consider settling down and raising a family, and right up until recently I never missed it. Maybe leakage radiation is softening up my brain, but I had begun to think of these furry and fishy Weskers as being a little like my own children, that I was somehow responsible for them.'

'We are all His children,' Father Mark said quietly.

'Well, here are some of His children that can't even imagine His existence,' Garth said, suddenly angry at himself for allowing gentler emotions to show through. Yet he forgot himself at once, leaning forward with the intensity of his feelings. 'Can't you realize the importance of this? Live with these Weskers awhile and you will discover a simple and happy life that matches the state of grace you people are always talking about. They get *pleasure* from their lives – and cause no one pain. By circumstances they have evolved on an almost barren world, so have never had a chance to grow out of a physical stone age culture. But mentally they are our match – or perhaps better. They have all learned my language so I can easily explain the many things they want to know. Knowledge and the gaining of knowledge gives them real satisfaction. They tend to be exasperating at times because every new fact must be related to the structure of all other things, but the more they learn the faster this process becomes. Some day they are going to be man's equal in every way, perhaps surpass us. If – would you do me a favour?'

'Whatever I can.'

'Leave them alone. Or teach them if you must – history and science, philosophy, law, anything that will help them face the realities of the greater universe they never even knew existed before. But don't confuse them with your hatreds and pain, guilt, sin, and punishment. Who knows the harm . . .'

'You are being insulting, sir!' the priest said, jumping to his feet. The top of his grey head barely came to the massive spaceman's chin, yet he showed no fear in defending what he believed. Garth, standing now himself, was no longer the penitent. They faced each other in anger, as men have always stood, unbending in the defence of that which they think right.

'Yours is the insult,' Garth shouted. 'The incredible egotism to feel that your derivative little mythology, differing only slightly from the thousands of others that still burden men, can do anything but confuse their still fresh minds! Don't you realize that they believe in truth – and have never heard of such a thing as a lie. They have not been trained yet to understand that other kinds of minds can think differently from theirs. Will you spare them this . . .?'

'I will do my duty which is His will, Mr Garth. These are God's creatures here, and they have souls. I cannot shirk my duty, which is to bring them His word, so that they may be saved and enter into the Kingdom of Heaven.'

When the priest opened the door the wind caught it and blew it wide. He vanished into the stormswept darkness and the door swung back and forth and a splatter of raindrops blew in. Garth's boots left muddy footprints when he closed the door, shutting out the sight of Itin sitting patiently and uncomplaining in the storm, hoping only that Garth might stop for a moment and leave with him some of the wonderful knowledge of which he had so much.

By unspoken consent that first night was never mentioned again. After a few days of loneliness, made worse because each knew of the other's proximity, they found themselves talking on carefully neutral grounds. Garth slowly packed and stowed away his stock and never admitted that his work was finished and he could leave at any time. He had a fair amount of interesting drugs and botanicals that would fetch a good price. And the Wesker Artefacts were sure to create a sensation in the sophisticated galactic market. Crafts on the planet here had been limited before his arrival, mostly pieces of carving painfully chipped into the hard wood with fragments of stone. He had supplied tools and a stock of raw metal from his own supplies, nothing more than that. In a few months the Weskers had not only learned to work with the new materials, but had translated their own designs and forms into the most alien – but most beautiful – artefacts that he had ever seen. All he had to do was release these on the market to create a primary demand, then return for a new supply. The Weskers wanted only books and tools and knowledge in return, and through their own efforts he knew they would pull themselves into the galactic union.

This is what Garth had hoped. But a wind of change was blowing through the settlement that had grown up around his ship. No longer was he the centre of attention and focal point of the village life. He had to grin when he thought of his fall from power; yet there was very little humour in the smile. Serious and attentive Weskers still took turns of duty as Knowledge Collectors, but their recording of dry facts was in sharp contrast to the intellectual hurricane that surrounded the priest.

Whereas Garth had made them work for each book and machine, the priest gave freely. Garth had tried to be progressive in his supply of knowledge, treating them as bright but unlettered children. He had wanted them to walk before they could run, to master one step before going on to the next.

Father Mark simply brought them the benefits of Christianity. The only physical work he required was the construction of a church, a place of worship and learning. More Weskers had appeared out of the limitless planetary swamps and within days the roof was up, supported on a framework of poles. Each morning the congregation worked a little while on the walls, then hurried inside to learn the all-promising, all-encompassing, all-important facts about the universe.

Garth never told the Weskers what he thought about their new interest, and this was mainly because they had never asked him. Pride or honour stood in the way of his grabbing a willing listener and pouring out his grievances. Perhaps it would have been different if Itin was on Collecting duty; he was the brightest of the lot; but Itin had been rotated the day after the priest had arrived and Garth had not talked to him since.

It was a surprise then when after seventeen of the trebly-long Wesker days, he found a delegation at his doorstep when he emerged after breakfast. Itin was their spokesman, and his mouth was open slightly. Many of the other Weskers had their mouths open as well, one even appearing to be yawning, clearly revealing the double row of sharp teeth and the purple-black throat. The mouths impressed Garth as to the seriousness of the meeting: this was the one Wesker expression he had learned

16

to recognize. An open mouth indicated some strong emotion; happiness, sadness, anger, he could never be really sure which. The Weskers were normally placid and he had never seen enough open mouths to tell what was causing them. But he was surrounded by them now.

'Will you help us, John Garth?' Itin said. 'We have a question.'

'I'll answer any question you ask,' Garth said, with more than a hint of misgiving. 'What is it?'

'Is there a God?'

'What do you mean by "God"?' Garth asked in turn. What should he tell them?

'God is our Father in Heaven, who made us all and protects us. Whom we pray to for aid, and if we are Saved will find a place . . .'

'That's enough,' Garth said. 'There is no God.'

All of them had their mouths open now, even Itin, as they looked at Garth and thought about his answer. The rows of pink teeth would have been frightening if he hadn't known these creatures so well. For one instant he wondered if perhaps they had been already indoctrinated and looked upon him as a heretic, but he brushed the thought away.

'Thank you,' Itin said, and they turned and left.

Though the morning was still cool, Garth noticed that he was sweating and wondered why.

The reaction was not long in coming. Itin returned that same afternoon. 'Will you come to the church?' he asked. 'Many of the things that we study are difficult to learn, but none as difficult as this. We need your help because we must hear you and Father Mark talk together. This is because he says one thing is true and you say another is true and both cannot be true at the same time. We must find out what is true.'

'I'll come, of course,' Garth said, trying to hide the sudden feeling of elation. He had done nothing, but the Weskers had come to him anyway. There could still be grounds for hope that they might yet be free.

It was hot inside the church, and Garth was surprised at the number of Weskers who were there, more than he had seen gathered at any one time before. There were many open mouths. Father Mark sat at a table covered with books. He looked unhappy but didn't say anything when Garth came in. Garth spoke first.

'I hope you realize this is their idea – that they came to me of their own free will and asked me to come here?'

'I know that,' the priest said resignedly. 'At times they can be very difficult. But they are learning and want to believe, and that is what is important.'

'Father Mark, Trader Garth, we need your help,' Itin said. 'You both know many things that we do not know. You must help us come to religion which is not an easy thing to do.' Garth started to say something, then changed his mind. Itin went on. 'We have read the bibles and all the books that Father Mark gave us, and one thing is clear. We have discussed this and we are all agreed. These books are very different from the ones that Trader Garth gave us. In Trader Garth's books there is the universe which we have not seen, and it goes on without God, for he is mentioned nowhere; we have searched very carefully. In Father Mark's books He is everywhere and nothing can go without Him. One of these must be right and the other must be wrong. We do not know how this can be, but after we find out which is right then perhaps we will know. If God does not exist . . .'

'Of course He exists, my children,' Father Mark said in a voice of heartfelt intensity. 'He is our Father in Heaven who has created us all. . . .'

'Who created God?' Itin asked and the murmur ceased and every one of the Weskers watched Father Mark intensely. He recoiled a bit under the impact of their eyes, then smiled.

'Nothing created God, since He is the Creator. He always was. . . .'

'If He always was in existence – why cannot the universe have always been in existence? Without having had a creator?' Itin broke in with a rush of words. The importance of the question was obvious. The priest answered slowly, with infinite patience.

'Would that the answers were that simple, my children. But even the scientists do not agree about the creation of the universe. While they doubt – we who have seen the light *know*.

We can see the miracle of creation all about us. And how can there be a creation without a Creator? That is He, our Father, our God in Heaven. I know you have doubts; that is because you have souls and free will. Still, the answer is so simple. Have faith, that is all you need. Just believe.'

'How can we believe without proof?'

'If you cannot see that this world itself is proof of His existence, then I say to you that belief needs no proof – if you have faith!'

A babble of voices arose in the room and more of the Wesker mouths were open now as they tried to force their thoughts through the tangled skein of words and separate the thread of truth.

'Can you tell us, Garth?' Itin asked, and the sound of his voice quieted the hubbub.

'I can tell you to use the scientific method which can examine all things – including itself – and give you answers that can prove the truth or falsity of any statement.'

'That is what we must do,' Itin said. 'We had reached the same conclusion.' He held a thick book before him and a ripple of nods ran across the watchers. 'We have been studying the bible as Father Mark told us to do, and we have found the answer. God will make a miracle for us, thereby proving that He is watching us. And by this sign we will know Him and go to Him.'

'That is the sin of false pride,' Father Mark said. 'God needs no miracles to prove His existence.'

'But *we* need a miracle!' Itin shouted, and though he wasn't human there was need in his voice. 'We have read here of many smaller miracles, loaves, fishes, wine, snakes – many of them, for much smaller reasons. Now all He need do is make a miracle and He will bring us all to Him – the wonder of an entire new world worshipping at His throne, as you have told us, Father Mark. And you have told us how important this is. We have discussed this and find that there is only one miracle that is best for this kind of thing.'

His boredom at the theological wrangling drained from Garth in an instant. He had not been really thinking or he would have realized where all this was leading. He could see the illustration in the bible where Itin held it open, and knew in advance what picture it was. He rose slowly from his chair, as if stretching, and turned to the priest behind him.

'Get ready!' he whispered. 'Get out the back and get to the ship; I'll keep them busy here. I don't think they'll harm me.'

'What do you mean . . .?' Father Mark asked, blinking in surprise.

'Get out, you fool!' Garth hissed. 'What miracle do you think they mean? What miracle is supposed to have converted the world to Christianity?'

'No!' Father Mark said. 'It cannot be. It just cannot be . . .!'

'GET MOVING!' Garth shouted, dragging the priest from the chair and hurling him towards the rear wall. Father Mark stumbled to a halt, turned back. Garth leaped for him, but it was already too late. The amphibians were small, but there was so many of them. Garth lashed out and his fist struck Itin, hurling him back into the crowd. The others came on as he fought his way towards the priest. He beat at them but it was like struggling against waves. The furry, musky bodies washed over and engulfed him. He fought until they tied him, and he still struggled until they beat on his head until he stopped. Then they pulled him outside where he could only lie in the rain and curse and watch.

Of course the Weskers were marvellous craftsmen, and everything had been constructed down to the last detail, following the illustration in the bible. There was the cross, planted firmly on the top of a small hill, the gleaming metal spikes, the hammer. Father Mark was stripped and draped in a carefully pleated loincloth. They led him out of the church.

At the sight of the cross he almost fainted. After that he held his head high and determined to die as he had lived, with faith.

Yet this was hard. It was unbearable even for Garth, who only watched. It is one thing to talk of crucifixion and look at the gentle carved bodies in the dim light of prayer. It is another to see a man naked, ropes cutting into his skin where he hangs from a bar of wood. And to see the needle-tipped spike raised and placed against the soft flesh of his palm, to see the hammer come back with the calm deliberation of an artisan's measured stroke. To hear the thick sound of metal penetrating flesh.

Then to hear the screams.

Few are born to be martyrs; Father Mark was not one of them. With the first blows, the blood ran from his lips where his clenched teeth met. Then his mouth was wide and his head strained back and the guttural horror of his screams sliced through the susurration of the falling rain. It resounded as a silent echo from the masses of watching Weskers, for whatever emotion opened their mouths was now tearing at their bodies with all its force, and row after row of gaping jaws reflected the crucified priest's agony.

Mercifully he fainted as the last nail was driven home. Blood ran from the raw wounds, mixing with the rain to drip faintly pink from his feet as the life ran out of him. At this time, somewhere at this time, sobbing and tearing at his own bonds, numbed from the blows on the head, Garth lost consciousness.

He awoke in his own warehouse and it was dark. Someone was cutting away the woven ropes they had bound him with. The rain still dripped and splashed outside.

'Itin,' he said. It could be no one else.

'Yes,' the alien voice whispered back. 'The others are all talking in the church. Lin died after you struck his head, and Inon is very sick. There are some that say you should be crucified too, and I think that is what will happen. Or perhaps killed by stoning on the head. They have found in the bible where it says . . .'

'I know.' With infinite weariness. 'An eye for an eye. You'll find lots of things like that once you start looking. It's a wonderful book.' His head ached terribly.

'You must go, you can get to your ship without anyone seeing you. There has been enough killing.' Itin as well, spoke with a new-found weariness.

Garth experimented, pulling himself to his feet. He

pressed his head to the rough wood of the wall until the nausea stopped. 'He's dead.' He said it as a statement, not a question.

'Yes, some time ago. Or I could not have come away to see you.'

'And buried of course, or they wouldn't be thinking about starting on me next.'

'And buried!' There was almost a ring of emotion in the alien's voice, an echo of the dead priest's. 'He is buried and he will rise on High. It is written and that is the way it will happen. Father Mark will be so happy that it has happened like this.' The voice ended in a sound like a human sob.

Garth painfully worked his way towards the door, leaning against the wall so he wouldn't fall.

'We did the right thing, didn't we?' Itin asked. There was no answer. 'He will rise up, Garth, won't he rise?'

Garth was at the door and enough light came from the brightly lit church to show his torn and bloody hands clutching at the frame. Itin's face swam into sight close to his, and Garth felt the delicate, many fingered hands with the sharp nails catch at his clothes.

'He will rise, won't he, Garth?'

'No,' Garth said. 'He is going to stay buried right where you put him. Nothing is going to happen because he is dead and he is going to stay dead.'

The rain runnelled through Itin's fur and his mouth was opened so wide that he seemed to be screaming into the night. Only with effort could he talk, squeezing out the alien thoughts in an alien language.

'Then we will not be saved? We will not become pure?'

'You were pure,' Garth said, in a voice somewhere between a sob and a laugh. 'That's the horrible ugly dirty part of it. You were pure. Now you are . . .'

'Murderers,' Itin said, and the water ran down from his lowered head and streamed away into the darkness.

II A.M.!!! the note blared at him, pinned to the upper right corner of his drawing board. MARTIN'S OFFICE!! He had lettered it himself with a number 7 brush, funereal india ink on harsh yellow paper, big letters, big words.

Big end to everything. Pachs tried to make himself believe that this was just another one of Martin's royal commands: a lecture, a chewing-out, a complaint. That's what he had thought when he had knocked out the reminder for himself, before Miss Finks' large, watery eyes had blinked at him and she had whispered hoarsely, 'It's on order, Mr Pachs, coming today, I saw the receipt on his desk. A Mark IX.' She had blinked moistly again, rolled her eyes towards the closed door of Martin's office then scurried away.

A Mark IX. He knew that it would have to come some day, knew without wanting to admit it, and had only been kidding himself when he said they couldn't do without him. His hands spread out on the board before him, old hands, networked wrinkles and dark liver spots, always stained a bit with ink and marked with a permanent callous on the inside of his index finger. How many years had he held a pencil or a brush there? He didn't want to remember. Too many, perhaps. . . . He clasped his hands tightly together, making believe he didn't see them shaking.

There was almost an hour left before he had to see Martin, plenty of time to finish up the story he was working on. He pulled the sheet of illustration board from the top of the pile and found the script. Page three of a thing called *Prairie Love* for the July issue of *Real Rangeland Romances*. Love books with their heavy copy were always a snap. By the time Miss Fink had typed in the endless captions and dialogue on her big flatbed varityper at least half of every panel was full. The script, panel one:

In house, Judy C/U cries and Robert in BG very angry.

A size three head for Judy in the foreground, he quickly

23

drew the right size oval in blue pencil, then a stick figure for Robert in the background. Arm raised, fist closed, to show anger. The Mark VIII Robot Comic Artist would do all the rest. Pachs slipped the sheet into the machine's holder – then quickly pulled it out again. He had forgotten the balloons. Sloppy, sloppy. He quickly blue-pencilled their outlines and V's for tails.

When he thumbed the switch the machine hummed to life, electronic tubes glowing inside its dark case. He punched the control button for the heads, first the girl – GIRL HEAD, FULL FRONT, SIZE THREE, SAD, HEROINE. Girls of course all had the same face in comic books, the HEROINE was just a note to the machine not to touch the hair. For a VILLAINESS it would be inked in black, all villainesses have black hair, just as all villains have moustaches as well as the black hair, to distinguish them from the hero. The machine buzzed and clattered to itself while it sorted through the stock cuts, then clicked and banged down a rubber stamp of the correct head over the blue circle he had drawn. MAN HEAD, FULL FRONT, SIZE SIX, SAD, HERO, brought a smaller stamp banging down on the other circle that topped the stick figure. Of course the script said *angry*, but that was what the raised fist was for, since there are only sad and happy faces in comics.

Life isn't that simple, he thought to himself, a very unoriginal idea that he usually brought out at least once a day while sitting at the machine. MAN FIGURE, BUSINESS SUIT, he set on the dial, then hit the DRAW button. The pen-tipped arm dropped instantly and began to quickly ink in a suited man's figure over the blue direction lines he had put down. He blinked and watched it industriously knocking in a wrinkle pattern that hadn't varied a stroke in fifty years, then a collar and tie and two swift neck lines to connect the neatly inked torso to the rubber-stamped head. The pen leaped out to the cuff end of the just-drawn sleeve and quivered there. A relay buzzed and a dusty red panel flashed INSTRUCTIONS PLEASE at him. With a savage jab he pushed the button labelled FIST. The light went out and the flashing pen drew a neat fist at the end of the arm.

Pachs looked at the neatly drawn panel and sighed. The girl wasn't unhappy enough; he dipped his crowquill into the

24

ink pot and knocked in two tears, one in the corner of each eye. Better. But the background was still pretty empty in spite of the small dictionary in each balloon. BALLOONS he punched automatically while he thought, and the machine pen darted down and inked the outlines of the balloons that held the lettering, ending each tail the correct distance from the speaker's mouth. A little background, it needed a touch. He pressed code 473 which he knew from long experience stood for HOME WINDOW WITH LACE CURTAINS. It appeared on the paper quickly, automatically scaled by the machine to be in perspective with the man's figure before it. Pachs picked up the script and read panel two:

Judy falls on couch Robert tries to console her mother rushes in angrily wearing apron.

There was a four-line caption in this panel and, after the three balloons had been lettered as well, the total space remaining was just about big enough for a single closeup, a small one. Pachs didn't labour this panel, as he might have, but took the standard way out. He was feeling tired today, very tired. HOUSE, SMALL, FAMILY produced a small cottage from which emerged the tails of the three balloons and let the damn reader figure out who was talking.

The story was finished just before eleven and he stacked the pages neatly, put the script into the file and cleaned the ink out of the pen in the Mark VIII; it always clogged if he left it to dry.

Then it was eleven and time to see Martin. Pachs fussed a bit, rolling down his sleeves and hanging his green eyeshade from the arm of his dazor lamp; yet the moment could not be avoided. Pulling his shoulders back a bit he went out past Miss Fink hammering away industriously on the varityper, and walked in through the open door to Martin's office.

'Come ON, Louis,' Martin wheedled into the phone in his most syrupy voice. 'If it's a matter of taking the word of some two-bit shoestring distributor in Kansas City, or of taking my word, who you gonna doubt? That's right . . . okay . . . right Louis. I'll call you back in the morning . . . right, you too . . . my best to Helen.' He banged the phone back onto the desk and glared up at Pachs with his hard beebee eyes.

'What do you want?'

'You told me you wanted to see me, Mr Martin.'

'Yeah, yeah,' Martin mumbled half to himself. He scratched flakes of dandruff loose from the back of his head with the chewed end of a pencil, and rocked from side to side in his chair.

'Business is business, Pachs, you know that, and expenses go up all the time. Paper – you know how much it costs a ton? So we gotta cut corners. . . .'

'If you're thinking of cutting my salary again, Mr Martin, I don't think I could . . . well, maybe not much. . . .'

'I'm gonna have to let you go, Pachs. I've bought a Mark IX to cut expenses and I already hired some kid to run it.'

'You don't have to do that, Mr Martin,' Pachs said hurriedly, aware that his words were tumbling one over the other and that he was pleading, but not caring. 'I could run the machine I'm sure, just give me a few days to catch on. . . .'

'Outta the question. In the first place I'm paying the kid beans because she's just a kid and that's the starting salary, and in the other place she's been to school about this thing and can really grind the stuff out. You know I'm no bastard, Pachs, but business is business. And I'll tell you what, this is only Tuesday and I'll pay you for the rest of the week. How's that? And you can take off right now.'

'Very generous, particularly after eight years,' Pachs said, forcing his voice to be calm.

'That's all right, it's the least I could do.' Martin was congenitally immune to sarcasm.

The lost feeling hit Pachs then, a dropping away of his stomach, a sensation that everything was over. Martin was back on the phone again and there was really nothing that Pachs could say. He walked out of the office, walking very straight, and behind him he heard the banging of Miss Fink's machine halt for an instant. He did not want to see her, to face those tender and damp eyes, not now. Instead of turning to go back to the studio, where he would have to pass her desk, he opened the hall door and stepped out. He closed it slowly behind him and stood with his back to it for an instant, until he realized it was frosted glass and she could see his figure from the inside: he moved hurriedly away.

26

There was a cheap bar around the corner where he had a beer every pay day, and he went there now. 'Good morning and top of the morning to you ... Mr Pachs,' the robot bartender greeted him with recorded celtic charm, hesitating slightly between the stock phrase and the search of the customer-tapes for his name. 'And will you be having the usual?'

'No I will not be having the usual, you plastic and gaspipe imitation of a cheap stage Irishman, I'll be having a double whiskey.'

'Sure and you are the card, sir,' the electronically affable bartender nodded, horsehair spitcurl bobbing, as it produced a glass and bottle and poured a carefully measured drink.

Pachs drank it in a gulp and the unaccustomed warmth burned through the core of cold indifference that he had been holding on to. Christ, it was all over, all over. They would get him now with their Senior Citizens' Home and all the rest, he was good as dead.

There are some things that don't bear thinking about. This was one. Another double whiskey followed the first, the money for this was no longer important because he would be earning no more after this week, and the unusual dose of alcohol blurred some of the pain. Now, before he started thinking about it too much, he had to get back to the office. Clean his personal junk out of the taboret and pick up his pay check from Miss Fink. It would be ready, he knew that; when Martin was through with you he liked to get you out of the way, quickly.

'Floor please?' the voice questioned from the top of the elevator.

'Go straight to hell!' he blurted out. He had never before realized how many robots there were around: Oh how he hated them today.

'I'm sorry, the firm is not in this building, have you consulted the registry?'

'Twenty-three,' he said and his voice quavered, and he was glad he was alone in the elevator. The doors closed.

There was a hall entrance to the studio and this door was standing open, he was halfway through it before he realized why – then it was too late to turn back. The Mark VIII that he had nursed along and used for so many years lay on its side in the corner, uprooted and very dusty on the side that had stood against the wall.

Good he thought to himself, and at the same time knew it was stupid to hate a machine, but still relishing the thought that it was being discarded too. In its place stood a columnar apparatus in a grey crackle cabinet. It reached almost to the ceiling and appeared as ponderous as a safe.

'It's all hooked up now, Mr Martin, ready to go with a hundred per cent lifetime guarantee as you know. But I'll just sort of preflight it for you and give you an idea just how versatile this versatile machine is.'

The speaker was dressed in grey coveralls of the identical colour as the machine's finish, and was pointing at it with a gleaming screwdriver. Martin watched, frowning, and Miss Fink fluttered in the background. There was someone else there, a thin young girl in a pink sweater who bovinely chewed at a cud of gum.

'Let's give Mark IX here a real assignment, Mr Martin. A cover for one of your magazines, something I bet you never thought a machine could tackle before, and normal machines can't. . . .'

'Fink!' Martin barked and she scrambled over with a sheet of illustration board and a small colour sketch.

'We got just one cover in the house to do, Mr Martin,' she said weakly. 'You okayed it for Mr Pachs to do. . . .'

'The hell with all that,' Martin growled, pulling it from her hand and looking at it closely. 'This is for our best book, do you understand that, and we can't have no hack horsing around with rubber stamps. Not on the cover of *Fighting Real War Battle Aces*.'

'You need not have the slightest worry, I assure you,' the man in the coveralls said, gently lifting the sketch from Martin's fingers. 'I'm going to show you the versatility of the Mark IX, something that you might find it impossible to believe until you see it in action. A trained operator can cut a Mark IX tape from a sketch or a description, and the results are always dramatic to say the least.' He seated himself at a console with typewriter keys that projected from the side of the machine, and while he typed a ribbon of punched tape collected in the basket at one side.

'Your new operator knows the machine code and breaks down any art concept into standard symbols, cut on tape. The tape can be examined or corrected, stored or modified and used over again if need be. There – I've recorded the essence of your sketch and now I have one more question to ask you – in what style would you like it to be done?'

Martin made a porcine interrogative sound.

'Startled aren't you, sir – well I thought you would be. The Mark IX contains style tapes of all the great masters of the Golden Age. You can have Kubert or Caniff, Giunta or Barry. For figure work – you can use Raymond, for your romances capture the spirit of Drake.'

'How's about Pachs?'

'I'm sorry, I'm afraid I don't know of . . .'

'A joke. Let's get going. Caniff, that's what I want to see.'

Pachs felt himself go warm all over, then suddenly cold. Miss Fink looked over and caught his eye, and looked down, away. He clenched his fists and shifted his feet to leave, but listened instead. He could not leave, not yet.

'. . . and the tape is fed into the machine, the illustration board centred on the impression table and the cycle button depressed. So simple, once a tape has been cut, that a child of three could operate it. A press on the button and just stand back. Within this genius of a machine the orders are being analysed and a picture built up. Inside the memory circuits are bits and pieces of every object that man has ever imagined or seen and drawn for his own edification. These are assembled in the correct manner in the correct proportions and assembled on the collator screen. When the final picture is complete the all-clear light flashes – there it goes – and we can examine the completed picture on the screen here.' Martin bent over and looked in through the hooded opening and exhaled through his nose.

'Just perfect, isn't it? But if for any reason the operator is dissatisfied the image can be changed now in any manner desired by manipulation of the editorial controls. And when satisfied the print button is depressed, the image is printed on a film of re-usable plastic sheet, charged electrostatically in order to pick up the powdered ink and then the picture is printed in a single stroke on to the paper below.'

A pneumatic groan echoed theatrically from the bowels of the machine as a rectangular box crept down on a shining plunger and pressed against the paper. It hissed and a trickle of vapour oozed out. The machine rose back to position and the man in the coveralls held up the paper, smiling.

'Now isn't that a fine piece of art?'

Martin grunted.

Pachs looked at it and couldn't take his eyes away: he was afraid he was going to be sick. The cover was not only good, it was good Caniff, just as the master might have drawn it himself. Yet the most horrible part was that it was Pachs' cover, his own layout. Improved. He had never been what might be called a tremendous artist, but he wasn't a bad artist. He did all right in comics, and during the good years he was on top of the pack. But the field kept shrinking and when the machines came in it went bust and there was almost no spot for an artist, just a job here and there as sort of layout boy and machine minder. He had taken that – how many years now? – because old and dated as his work was he was still better than any machine that drew heads with a rubber stamp.

Not any more. He could not even pretend to himself any more that he was needed, or even useful.

The machine was better.

He realized then that he had been clenching his fists so tightly that his nails had sunk into the flesh of his palms. He opened and rubbed them together and knew that they were shaking badly. The Mark IX was turned off and they were all gone: he could hear Miss Fink's machine takking away in the outer office. The little girl was telling Martin about the special supplies she would need to buy to operate the machine, and when Pachs closed the connecting door he cut off the grumbling reply about extra expenses not being mentioned.

Pachs warmed his fingers in his armpits until the worst of the tremors stopped. Then he carefully pinned a sheet of paper on to his old drawing board and adjusted the light so it would not be in his eyes. With measured strokes he ruled out a standard comic page and separated it into six panels, making the sixth panel a big one, stretching the width of the page. He worked steadily at the pencilling, stopping only once to stretch his back and walk over to the window and look out. Then he went back to the board and as the afternoon light faded he finished the inking. Very carefully he washed off his battered – but still favourite – Windsor & Newton brush and slipped it back into the spring holder.

There was a bustle in the outer office and it sounded like Miss Fink getting ready to leave, or maybe it was the new girl coming back with the supplies. In any case it was late, and he had to go now.

Quickly, before he could change his mind, he ran full tilt at the window, his weight bursting through the glass, and hurtled the twenty-three storeys to the street below.

Miss Fink heard the breaking glass and screamed, then screamed louder when she came into the room. Martin, complaining about the noise, followed her, but shut up when he saw what had happened. A bit of glass crunched under his shoes when he looked out of the window. The doll-like figure of Pachs was visible in the centre of the gathering crowd, sprawled from sidewalk to street and bent at an awful angle as it followed the step of the curb.

'Oh God, Mr Martin. Oh God look at this . . .' Miss Fink wailed.

Martin went and stood next to her in front of the drawing board and looked at the page still pinned there. It was neatly done, well drawn and carefully inked.

In the first panel was a self portrait of Pachs working on a page, bent over this same drawing board. In the second panel he was sitting back and washing out his brush, in the third standing. In the fourth panel the artist stood before the window, nicely rendered in chiaroscuro with backlighting. Five was a forced perspective shot from above, down the vertical face of the building with the figure hurtling through the air towards the pavement below.

In the last panel, in clear and horrible detail, the old man was bent, broken and bloody over the wrecked fender of the car that was parked there: the spectators looked on horrified.

'Look at that will you,' Martin said disgustedly, tapping the drawing with his thumb. 'When he went out the window he missed the car by a good two yards. Didn't I always tell you he was no good on getting the details right?'

RESCUE OPERATION

'Pull! Pull steadily . . . !' Dragomir shouted, clutching at the tarry cords of the net. Beside him in the hot darkness Pribislav Polašek grunted with effort as he heaved on the wet strands. The net was invisible in the black water, but the blue light trapped in it rose closer and closer to the surface.

'Oh dear God – it's slipping. . . .' Pribislav groaned and clutched the rough gunwale of the little boat. For a single instant he could see the blue light on the helmet, a face plate and the suited body that faded into blackness – then it slipped free of the net. He had just a glimpse of a dark shape on the back before it was gone. 'Did you see it?' he asked. 'Just before he fell he waved his hand.'

'How can I know – the hand moved, it could have been the net, or he might still be alive?' Dragomir had his face bent almost to the glassy surface of the water, but there was nothing more to be seen. 'He might be alive.'

The two fishermen sat back in the boat and stared at each other in the harsh light of the hissing acetylene lamp in the bow. They were very different men, yet greatly alike in their stained, baggy trousers and faded cotton shirts. Their hands were deeply wrinkled and calloused from a lifetime of hard labour, their thoughts slowed by the rhythm of work and years.

'We cannot get him up with the net,' Dragomir finally said, speaking first as always.

'Then we will need help,' Pribislav added. 'We have anchored the buoy here, we can find the spot again.'

'Yes, we need help.' Dragomir opened and closed his large hands, then leaned over to bring the rest of the net into the boat. 'The diver, the one who stays with the widow Korenč, he will know what to do. His name is Kukovič and Petar said he is a doctor of science from the university in Ljubljana.'

They went to their oars and sent the heavy boat steadily

33

over the glasslike water of the Adriatic. Before they had reached shore the sky was light and when they tied to the sea wall in Brbinj the sun was above the horizon.

Jože Kukovič looked at the rising ball of the sun, already hot on his skin, yawned and stretched. The widow shuffled out with his coffee, mumbled good morning and put it on the stone rail of the porch. He pushed the tray aside and sat down next to it, then emptied the coffee from the small, long-handled pot into his cup. The thick Turkish coffee would wake him up, in spite of the impossible hour. From the rail he had a view down the unpaved and dusty street to the port, already stirring to life. Two women, with the morning's water in brass pots balanced on their heads, stopped to talk. The peasants were bringing in their produce for the morning market, baskets of cabbages and potatoes and trays of tomatoes, strapped onto tiny donkeys. One of them brayed, a harsh noise that sawed through the stillness of the morning, bouncing echoes from the yellowed buildings. It was hot already. Brbinj was a town at the edge of nowhere, locked between empty ocean and barren hills, asleep for centuries and dying by degrees. There were no attractions here – if you did not count the sea. But under the flat, blue calm of the water was another world that Jože loved. Cool shadows, deep valleys, more alive than all the sunblasted shores that surrounded it. Excitement too: just the day before, too late in the afternoon to really explore it, he had found a Roman galley half-buried in the sand. He would get into it today, the first human in two thousand years, and heaven alone knew what he would find there. In the sand about it had been shards of broken amphorae, there might be whole ones inside the hull. Sipping happily at his coffee, he watched the small boat tying up in the harbour, and wondered why the two fishermen were in such a hurry. They were almost running, and no one ran here in the summer, coming up his street. Stopping below his porch the biggest one called up to him.

'Doctor, may we come up? There is something urgent.'

'Yes, of course.' He was surprised and wondered if they took him for a physician.'

Dragomir shuffled forward and did not know where to begin. He pointed out over the ocean.

34

'It fell, out there last night, we saw it, a *sputnik* without a doubt.'

'A traveller?' Jože Kukovič wrinkled his forehead, not quite sure that he heard right. When the locals were excited it was hard to follow their dialect. For such a small country Yugoslavia was cursed with a multitude of tongues.

'No, it was not a *putnik*, but a *sputnik*, one of the Russian space ships.'

'Or an American one,' Pribislav spoke for the first time, but he was ignored.

Jože smiled and sipped his coffee. 'Are you sure it wasn't a meteorite you saw? There is always a heavy meteor shower this time of the year.'

'A *sputnik*.' Dragomir insisted stolidly. 'The ship fell far out in the *Jadransko More* and vanished, we saw that. But the space pilot came down almost on top of us, into the water. . . .'

'The WHAT?' Jože gasped, jumping to his feet and knocking the coffee tray to the floor. The brass tray clanged and rattled in circles, unnoticed. 'There was a man in this thing – and he got clear?'

Both fishermen nodded at the same time and Dragomir continued. 'We saw this light fall from the *sputnik* when it went overhead and drop into the water. We couldn't see what it was, just a light, and we rowed there as fast as we could. It was still sinking and we dropped a net and managed to catch him. . . .'

'You have the pilot?'

'No, but once we pulled him close enough to the surface to see he was in a heavy suit, with a window like a diving suit, and there was something on his back that might have been like your tanks there.'

'He waved his hand,' Pribislav insisted.

'He might have waved a hand, we could not be sure. We came back for help.'

The silence lengthened and Jože realized that he was the help that they needed, and that they had turned the responsibility over to him. What should he do first? The astronaut might have his own oxygen tanks, Jože had no real idea what provisions were made for water landings, but if there were oxygen the man might still be alive.

35

Jože paced the floor while he thought, a short, square figure in khaki shorts and sandals. He was not handsome, his nose was too big and his teeth were too obvious for that, but he generated a certainty of power. He stopped and pointed to Pribislav.

'We're going to have to get him out. You can find the spot again?'

'A buoy.'

'Good. And we may need a doctor. You have none here, but is there one in Osor?'

'Doctor Bratoš, but he is very old. . . .'

'As long as he is still alive, we'll have to get him. Can anyone in this town drive an automobile?'

The fishermen looked towards the roof and concentrated, while Jože controlled his impatience.

'Yes, I think so,' Dragomir finally said. 'Petar was a *partizan*. . . .'

'That's right,' the other fisherman finished the thought. 'He has told many times how they stole German trucks and how he drove . . .'

'Well then, one of you get this Petar and give him these keys to my car, it's a German car so he should be able to manage. Tell him to bring the doctor back at once.'

Dragomir took the keys, but handed them to Pribislav who ran out.

'Now let's see if we can get the man up,' Jože said, grabbing his scuba gear and leading the way towards the boat.

They rowed, side by side, though Dragomir's powerful strokes did most of the work.

'How deep is the water out here?' Jože asked. He was already dripping with sweat as the sun burned on his bare back.

'The Kvarnerič is deeper up by Rab, but we were fishing off Trstenik and the bottom is only about four fathoms there. We're coming to the buoy.'

'Seven metres, it shouldn't be too hard to find him.' Jože kneeled in the bottom of the boat and slipped into the straps of the scuba. He buckled it tight, checked the valves, then turned to the fisherman before he bit onto the mouthpiece. 'Keep the boat near this buoy and I'll use it for a guide while I search. If I need a line or any help I'll surface over the astronaut, then you can bring the boat to me.'

He turned on the oxygen and slipped over the side, the cool water rising up his body as he sank below the surface. With a powerful kick he started towards the bottom, following the dropping line of the buoy rope. Almost at once he saw the man, spread-eagled on the white sand below.

Jože swam down, making himself stroke smoothly in spite of his growing excitement. Details were clearer as he dropped lower. There were no identifying marks on the pressure suit, it might be either American or Russian. It was a hard suit, metal or reinforced plastic, and painted green, with a single, flat faceplate in the helmet.

Because distance and size are so deceptive under water, Jože was on the sand next to the figure before he realized it was less than four feet long. He gasped and almost lost his mouthpiece.

Then he looked into the faceplate and saw that the creature inside was not human.

Jože coughed a bit and blew out a stream of bubbles: he had been holding his breath without realizing it. He just floated there, paddling slowly with his hands to stay in position, looking at the face within the helmet.

It was as still as a waxen cast, green wax with a roughened surface, slit nostrils, slit mouth and large eyeballs unseen but prominent as they pushed up against the closed lids. The arrangement of features was roughly human, but no human being ever had skin this colour or had a pulpy crest like this one, partially visible through the face plate, growing up from above the closed eyes. Jože stared down at the suit, made of some unknown material, and at the compact atmosphere re-generation apparatus on the alien's back. What kind of atmosphere? He looked back at the creature's face and saw that the eyes were open and the thing was watching him.

Fear was his first reaction; he shot back in the water like a startled fish then, angry at himself, came forward again. The alien slowly raised one arm, then dropped it limply. Jože looked through the faceplate and saw that the eyes were closed again. The alien was alive, but unable to move, perhaps it was injured and in pain. The wreck of the creature's ship showed

37

that something had been wrong with the landing. Reaching under as gently as he could he cradled the tiny body in his arms, trying to ignore a feeling of revulsion when the cold fabric of the thing's suit touched his bare arms. It was only metal or plastic, he had to be a scientist about this. When he lifted up the eyes still did not open and he bore the limp and almost weightless form up to the surface.

'You great stupid clumsy clod of a peasant, help me,' he shouted, spitting out his mouthpiece and treading water on the surface, but Dragomir only shook his head in terror and retreated to the point of the bow when he saw what the physicist had borne up from below.

'It is a creature from another world and cannot harm you!' Jože insisted but the fisherman would not approach. Jože cursed aloud and only managed with great difficulty to get the alien into the boat, then climbed in after him. Though he was twice Jože's size threats of violence drove Dragomir to the oars. But he used the farthest set of tholepins, even though it made rowing much more difficult. Jože dropped his scuba gear into the bottom of the boat and looked more closely at the drying fabric of the alien spacesuit. His fear of the unknown was forgotten in his growing enthusiasm. He was a nuclear physicist, but he remembered enough of his chemistry and mechanics to know that this material was compeletely impossible – by Earth's standards. Light green, it was hard as steel over the creature's limbs and torso, yet was soft and bent easily at the joints as he proved by lifting and dropping the limp arm. His eyes went down the alien's tiny figure: there was a thick hardness about the middle, roughly where a human waist would be, and hanging from this was a bulky container, like an oversize sporran. The suiting continued without an apparent seam – but the right leg! It was squeezed in and crushed as though it had been grabbed by a giant pliers. Perhaps this explained the creature's lack of motion. Could it be hurt? In pain?

Its eyes were open again and Jože realized in sudden horror that the helmet was filled with water. It must have leaked in, the thing was drowning. He grabbed at the helmet, seeing if it would screw off, tugging at it in panic while the great eyes rolled up towards him.

Then he forced himself to think, and shakingly let go. The alien was still quiet, eyes open, no bubbles apparently coming from lips or nose. Did it breathe? Had the water leaked in – or was it possible it had always been there? Was it water? Who knew what alien atmosphere it might breathe, methane, chlorine, sulphur dioxide – why not water? The liquid was inside, surely enough, the suit wasn't leaking and the creature seemed unchanged.

Jože looked up and saw that Dragomir's panicked strokes had brought them into the harbour already, and that a crowd was waiting on the shore.

The boat almost overturned as Dragomir leaped up onto the harbour wall, kicking backward in his panic. They drifted away and Jože picked the mooring line from the floor boards and coiled it in his hands. 'Here,' he shouted, 'catch this. Tie it onto the ring there.'

No one heard him, or if they heard, did not want to admit it. They stared down at the green-cased figure lying in the stern-sheets and a rustle of whispering blew across them like wind among pine boughs. The women clutched their hands to their breasts, crossing themselves.

'Catch this,' Jože said through clenched teeth, forcing himself to keep his temper. He hurled the rope onto the stones and they shied away from it. A youth grabbed it and slowly threaded it through the rusty ring, hands shaking and head tilted to one side, his mouth drooped in a permanent gape. He was feeble-minded, too simple to understand what was going on: he simply obeyed the shouted order.

'Help me get this thing ashore,' Jože called out, and even before the words were out of his mouth he realized the futility of the request. The peasants shuffled backwards, a blank-faced mob sharing the same fear of the unknown, the women like giant, staring dolls in their knee-length flaring skirts, black stockings and high felt shoes. He would have to do it himself. Balancing in the rocking boat he cradled the alien in his arms and lifted it carefully up onto the rough stone of the harbour wall. The circle of watchers pushed back even farther, some of the women choking off screams and running back to their houses, while the men muttered louder: Jože ignored them.

These people were going to be of no help to him – and they might cause trouble. His own room would be safest, he doubted if they would bother him there. He had just picked up the alien when a newcomer pushed through the watchers.

'There – what is that? Mary Mother of God – a *vrag*!' The old priest pointed in horror at the alien in Jože's arms and backed away, fumbling for his crucifix.

'Enough of your superstition!' Jože snapped. 'This is no devil but a sentient creature, a traveller. Now get out of my way.'

He pushed forward and they fled before him. Jože moved as quickly as he could without appearing to hurry, leaving the crowd behind. There was a slapping of quick footsteps, and he looked over his shoulders; it was the priest, Father Perc. His stained cassock flapped and his breath whistled in his throat with the unaccustomed exertion.

'Tell me, what are you doing . . . Doctor Kukovič? What is that . . . thing? Tell me. . . .'

'I told you. A traveller. Two of the local fishermen saw something come out from the sky and crash. This – alien came from it.' Jože spoke as calmly as possible. There might be trouble with the people, but not if the priest were on his side. 'It is a creature from another world, a water-breathing animal, and it's hurt. We must help it.'

Father Perc scrambled along sideways as he looked with obvious distaste at the motionless alien. 'It is wrong,' he mumbled, 'this is something unclean, *zao duh*. . . .'

'Neither demon nor devil, can't you get that through your mind. The Church recognizes the possibility of creatures from other planets – the Jesuits even argue about it – so why can't you? Even the Pope believes there is life on other worlds.'

'Does he? Does he?' the old man asked, blinking with red-rimmed eyes.

Jože brushed by him and up the steps to the widow Korenč's house. She was nowhere in sight as he went into his room and gently lowered the still-unconscious form of the alien onto his bed. The priest stopped in the doorway, quivering fingers on his rosary, uncertain. Jože stood over the bed, opening and closing his hands, just as unsure. What could he do? The creature was wounded, perhaps dying, something must be done. But what? The distant droning whine of a car's engine pushed into the hot room and he almost sighed with relief. It was his car, he recognized the sound, and it would be bringing the doctor. The car stopped outside and the doors slammed, but no one appeared. Jože waited tensely, realizing that the townspeople must be talking to the doctor, telling him what had happened. A slow minute passed, and Jože started from the room, but stopped before he passed the priest, still standing just inside the door. What in hell was keeping them: his window faced on an alleyway and he could not see the street in front of the building. Then the outside door opened and he could hear the widow's whispered voice. 'In there, straight through.'

There were two men, both dusty from the road. One was obviously the doctor, a short and dumpy man clutching a worn black bag, his bald head beaded with sweat. Next to him was a young man, tanned and windburned, dressed like the other fishermen: this must be Petar the ex-partizan.

It was Petar who went to the bed first, the doctor just stood clutching onto his bag and blinking about at the room.

'What is this thing?' Petar asked, then bent over, hands on his knees, to stare in through the faceplate. 'Whatever it is, it sure is ugly.'

'I don't know. It's from another planet, that's the only thing I know. Now move aside so that the doctor can look.' Jože waved and the physician moved reluctantly forward. 'You must be Dr. Bratoš. I'm Kukovič, professor of nuclear physics at the university in Ljubljana.' Perhaps waving around a little prestige might get this man's reluctant co-operation.

'Yes, how do you do. Very pleased to meet you professor, an honour I assure you. But what is it that you wish me to do, I do not understand?' He shook ever so lightly as he spoke and Jože realized that the man was very old, well into his eighties or more. He would have to be patient.

'This alien – whatever it is – is injured and unconscious. We must do what we can to save its life.'

'But what can I do? The thing is sealed in a metal garment –

41

look it is filled with water – I am a doctor, a medical man, but not for animals, creatures like that.'

'Neither am I, doctor – no one on earth is. But we must do our best. We must get the suit off the alien and then discover what we can do to help.'

'It is impossible! The fluid inside of it, it will run out.'

'Obviously, so we will have to take precaution. We will have to determine what the liquid is, then get more of it and fill the bathtub in the next room. I have been looking at the suit and the helmet seems to be a separate piece, clamped into position. If we loosen the clamps we should be able to get our sample.'

For precious seconds Dr Bratoš stood there, nibbling at his lips, before he spoke. 'Yes, we could do that, I suppose we could, but what could we catch the sample in? This is most difficult and irregular.'

'It doesn't make any damn difference what we catch the sample in,' Jože snapped, frustration pushing at his carefully held control. He turned to Petar who was standing silently by, smoking a cigarette in his cupped hand. 'Will you help? Get a soup plate, anything, from the kitchen.'

Petar simply nodded and left. There were muffled complaints from the widow, but he was back quickly with her best pot.

'That's good,' Jože said, lifting the alien's head, 'now, slide it under here.' With the pot in position he twisted one of the clamps; it snapped open but nothing else happened. A hairline opening was visible at the junction, but it stayed dry. But when Jože opened the second clamp there was a sudden gush of clear liquid under pressure, and before he fumbled the clamp shut again the pot was half full. He lifted the alien again and, without being told, Petar pulled the pot free and set it on the table by the window. 'It's hot,' he said.

Jože touched the outside of the container. 'Warm not hot, about one hundred-twenty degrees I would guess. A hot ocean on a hot planet.'

'But . . . it is water?' Doctor Bratoš asked haltingly.

'I suppose it is – but aren't you the one to find out? Is it fresh water or sea water?'

'I'm no chemist . . . how can I tell . . . it is very complicated.'

Petar laughed and took Jože's waterglass from the nightstand. 'That's not so hard to find out,' he said, and dipped it into the pot. He raised the half-filled glass, sniffed at it, then took a sip and puckered his lips. 'Tastes like ordinary sea water to me, but there's another taste, sort of bitter.'

Jože took the glass from him. 'This could be dangerous,' the doctor protested, but they ignored him. Yes, salt water, hot salt water with a sharpness to it. 'It tastes like more than a trace of iodine. Can you test for the presence of iodine, doctor.'

'Here . . . no, it is quite complicated. In the laboratory with the correct equipment. . . . His voice trailed off as he opened his bag on the table and groped through it. He brought his hand out empty. 'In the laboratory.'

'We have no laboratory or any other assistance, doctor. We will have to be satisfied with what we have here, ordinary sea water will have to do.'

'I'll get a bucket and fill the tub,' Petar said.

'Good. But don't fill the bathtub yet. Bring the water into the kitchen and we'll heat it, then pour it in.'

'Right.' Petar brushed past the silent and staring priest and was gone. Jože looked at Father Perc and thought of the people of the village.

'Stay here, doctor,' he said. 'This alien is your patient and I don't think anyone other than you should come near. Just sit by him.'

'Yes, of course, that is correct,' Doctor Bratoš said relievedly, pulling the chair over and sitting down.

The breakfast fire was still burning in the big stove and flamed up when Jože slid in more sticks. On the wall hung the big copper wash tub and he dropped it onto the stove with a clang. Behind him the widow's bedroom door opened, but slammed shut again when he turned. Petar came in with a bucket of water and poured it into the tub.

'What are the people doing?' Jože asked.

'Just milling about and bothering each other. They won't be any trouble. If you're worried about them I can drive back to Osor and bring the police, or telephone someone.'

43

'No, I should have thought of that earlier. Right now I need you here. You're the only one who isn't either senile or ignorant.'

Petar smiled. 'I'll get some more water.'

The bathtub was small and the washtub big. When the heated water was dumped in it filled it more than half way, enough to cover the small alien. There was a drain from the bathtub but no faucets: it was usually filled with a hose from the sink. Jože picked up the alien, cradling it like a child in his arms, and carried it into the bath. The eyes were open again, following his every movement, but making no protest. He lowered the creature gently into the water, then straightened a moment and took a deep breath. 'Helmet first, then we'll try to figure out how the suit opens.' He bent and slowly twisted the clamps.

With all four clamps open the helmet moved freely. He opened it a wide crack, ready to close it quickly if there were any signs of trouble. The ocean water would be flowing in now, mixing with the alien water, yet the creature made no complaint. After a minute Jože slowly pulled the helmet off, cradling the alien's head with one hand so that it would not bump to the bottom of the tub.

Once the helmet was clear the pulpy crest above the eyes sprang up like a coxcomb, reaching up over the top of the green head. A wire ran from the helmet to a shiny bit of metal on one side of the creature's skull. There was an indentation there and Jože slowly pulled a metal plug out, perhaps an earphone of some kind. The alien was opening and closing its mouth, giving a glimpse of bony yellow ridges inside, and a low humming could be heard.

Petar pressed his ear against the outside of the metal tube. 'The thing is talking or something, I can hear it.'

'Let me have your stethoscope, doctor,' Jože said, but when the doctor did not move he dug it from the bag himself. Yes – when he pressed it to the metal he could hear a rising and falling whine, speech of some kind.

'We can't possibly understand him – not yet,' he said, handing the stethoscope back to the doctor who took it automatically. 'We had better try to get the suit off.'

44

There were no seams or fastenings visible, nor could Jože find anything when he ran his fingers over the smooth surface. The alien must have understood what they were doing because it jerkingly raised one hand and fumbled at the metal sealing ring about the collar. With a liquid motion the suit split open down the front, the opening bifurcated and ran down each leg. There was a sudden welling of blue liquid from the injured leg.

Jože had a quick glimpse of green flesh, strange organs, then he spun about. 'Quick, doctor – your bag. The creature is hurt, that fluid might be blood, we have to help it.'

'What can I do?' Doctor Bratoš said, unmoving. 'Drugs, antiseptics – I might kill it – we know nothing of its body chemistry.'

'Then don't use any of those. This is a traumatic injury, you can bind it up, stop the bleeding, can't you?'

'Of course, of course,' the old man said, and at last his hands had familiar things to do, extracting bandages and sterile gauze from his bag, tape and scissors.

Jože reached into the warm and now murky water and forced himself to reach under the leg and grasp the hot, green flesh. It was strange – but not terrible. He lifted the limb free of the water and they saw a crushed gap oozing a thick blue fluid. Petar turned away, but the doctor put on a pad of gauze and tightened the bandages about it. The bleeding seemed to stop. The alien was fumbling at the discarded suit beside it in the tub, twisting its leg in Jože's grip. He looked down and saw it take something from the sporran container. Its mouth was moving again, he could hear the dim buzz of its voice.

'What is it? What do you want?' Jože asked.

It was holding the object across its chest now with both hands: it appeared to be a book of some kind. It might be a book, it might be anything. Yet it was covered in a shiny substance with dark markings on it, and at the edge seemed to be made of many sheets bound together. It could be a book. The leg was twisting now in Jože's grasp and the alien's mouth was open wider, as if it were shouting.

'The bandage will get wet if we put it back into the water,' the doctor said.

'Can't you wrap adhesive tape over it, seal it in?'

'In my bag – I'll need some more.'

While they talked the alien began to rock back and forth, splashing water from the tub, pulling its leg from Jože's grasp. It still held the book in one thin, multi-fingered hand, but with the other one it began to tear at the bandages on its leg.

'It's hurting itself, stop it, this is terrible,' the doctor said, recoiling from the tub. Jože snatched a piece of wrapping paper from the floor.

'You fool! You incredible fool!' he shouted. 'These compresses you used – they're impregnated with sulfanilamide.'

'I always use them, they're the best, American, they prevent wound infection.'

Jože pushed him aside and plunged his arms into the tub to tear the bandages free, but the alien reared up out of his grasp sitting up above the water, its mouth gaping wide. Its eyes were open and staring and Jože recoiled as a stream of water shot from its mouth. There was a gargling sound as the water died to a trickle, and then, as the first air touched the vocal cords, a rising, howling scream of pain. It echoed from the plaster ceiling, an inhuman agony as the creature threw its arms wide, then fell face forward into the water. It did not move again and, without examining it, Jože knew it was dead.

One arm was twisted back, out of the tub, still grasping the book. Slowly the fingers loosened, and while Jože looked on numbly, unable to move, the book thudded to the floor.

'Help me,' Petar said, and Jože turned to see that the doctor had fallen and Petar was kneeling over him. 'He fainted, or a heart attack. What do we do?'

His anger was forgotten as Jože kneeled. The doctor seemed to be breathing regularly and his face wasn't flushed, so perhaps it was only a fainting spell. The eyelids fluttered. The priest brushed by and looked down over Jože's shoulder.

Doctor Bratoš opened his eyes, looking back and forth at the faces bent over him. 'I'm sorry . . .' he said thickly, then the eyes closed again as if to escape the sight of them.

Jože stood, and found that he was trembling. The priest was gone. Was it all over? Perhaps they might never have saved the alien, but they should have done better than this. Then he saw the wet spot on the floor and realized the book was gone.

'Father Perc!' he shouted, crying it out like an insult. The man had taken the book, the priceless book!

Jože ran out into the hall and saw the priest coming from the kitchen. His hands were empty. With sudden fear Jože knew what the old man had done and brushed past him into the kitchen and ran to the stove, hurling open the door.

There, among the burning wood, lay the book. It was steaming, almost smoking as it dried, lying open. It was obviously a book, there were marks on the pages, pictures of some kind. He turned to grab up the shovel and behind him the fire exploded, sending a white flame across the room. It had almost caught him in the face, but he did not think of that. Pieces of burning wood lay on the floor, and inside the stove there was only the remains of the original fire. Whatever substance the book had been made of was highly inflammable once it had dried out.

'It was evil,' the priest said from the doorway. 'A *zao duh*, an abomination with a book of evil. We have been warned, such things have happened before on earth, and always the faithful must fight back. . . .'

Petar pushed in roughly past him and helped Jože to a chair, brushing the hot embers from his bare skin. Jože had not felt their burn, all he was aware of was an immense weariness.

'Why here?' he asked. 'Of all places in the world why here? A few more degrees to the west and the creature would have come down near Trieste with surgeons, hospitals, men, facilities. Or if it had just stayed on this course a little longer, it could have seen the lights, it would have landed at Rijeka. Something could have been done. But why *here*?' He surged to his feet, shaking his fist at nothing – and at everything.

'Here, in this superstition-ridden, simple-minded backwater of the world! What kind of world do we live in where there is a five-million-volt electron accelerator not a hundred miles from primitive stupidity. That this creature should come so far, come so close . . . why, why?'

Why?

He slumped back into the chair again feeling older than he

had ever felt before and tired beyond measure. What could they have learned from the book. . . ?

He sighed, and the sigh came from so deep within him that his whole body trembled as though shaken by an awful fever.

'What is space like? How do the naked stars really look? Those are hard questions to answer.' Captain Jonathan Bork looked around at the eager, intent faces waiting for his words, then dropped his eyes to his space-tanned hands on the table before him.

'Sometimes it's like falling into a million-mile pit, other times you feel like a fly in the spider web of eternity, naked under the stars. And the stars are so different – no flickering, you know, just the tiniest spots of solid light.'

Even as he told them he cursed himself a thousand times for the liar he was. Capt. Bork, spaceship pilot. The single man privileged to see the stars in the space between worlds. And after five round trips to Mars, he had no idea of what it was really like out there. His body piloted the ship, but Jonathan Bork had never seen the inside of a ship's control room.

Not that he ever dared admit it aloud. When people asked him what it was like he told them – using one of the carefully memorized speeches from the textbooks.

With an effort he pulled his mind away from the thought and back to the table surrounded by guests and relatives. The dinner was in his honour so he tried to live up to it. The brandy helped. He finished most of it, then excused himself as soon as he could.

The family house was old enough to have a pocket-sized backyard. He went there, alone, and put his back against the dark building still warm from the heat of the day. The unaccustomed brandy felt good, and when he looked up the stars wheeled in circles until he closed his eyes.

Stars. He had always looked at the stars. From the time he had been a child they had been his interest and his drive. Everything he had ever done or studied had that one purpose behind it. To be one of the select few to fly the space lanes. A pilot.

He had entered the academy when he was seventeen, the

minimum age. By the time he was eighteen he knew the whole thing was a fake.

He had tried hard to ignore the truth, to find some other explanation. But it was no good. Everything he knew, everything he was taught in the school added up to one thing. And *that* was an impossible conclusion.

It was inescapable and horrible so finally he had put it to the test. It happened in physiology class, where they were working out problems in relation to orientation and consciousness in acceleration, using Paley's theorem. He had raised his hand timidly, but Eagle-eye Cherniki had spotted it and growled him to his feet. Once he was committed the words came out in a rush.

'Professor Cherniki, if we accept Paley's theorem, in a problem like this with only minimal escape-G, we go well below the consciousness threshold. And the orientation factor as well, it seems to me . . . that, well . . .'

'Mr Bork, just what are you trying to say?' Cherniki's voice had the cold incision of a razor's edge.

Jon took the plunge. 'There can be only one conclusion. Any pilot who takes off in a ship will be knocked out or unable to orientate enough to work the controls.'

The classroom rocked with laughter and Jon felt his face warm and redden. Even Cherniki allowed himself a cold grin when he answered.

'Very good. But if what you say is true, then it is impossible to fly in space – and we do it every day. I think you will find that in the coming semester we will go into the question of changing thresholds under stress. That should—'

'No, sir,' Jon broke in. 'The texts do *not* answer this question – if anything they avoid it. I've read every text for this course as well as other related texts—'

'Mr Bork, are you calling me a liar?' Cherniki's voice was as frigid as his eyes. A dead hush fell over the classroom. 'You are dismissed from this class. Go to your quarters and remain there until you are sent for.'

Trying not to stumble, Jon went across the room and out the

door. Every eye was fixed on him and he felt like a prisoner on the last mile. Instead of getting an answer to his question it looked as if he had got himself in deep trouble. Sitting in his room he tried not to think of the consequences.

He had never been certain he could get into pilot training – even though it had been his only ambition. Just about one out of 100 made it that far, the rest ending up in the thousand other jobs of the space fleet. Very few washed completely out of the Academy; the entrance requirements were so high that deadheads never got that far. Of course, there were exceptions – and it was beginning to look like he was one of them.

When the intercom finally called him to the president's office he was almost ready for it. He still jumped when it barked for him then he got up quickly and left taking the elevator to the executive level. The cold-faced secretary nodded him in, and he was alone with the Admiral.

Admiral Sikelm had retired from active service when he took over the presidency of the Academy. He had never lost the manner or voice of command and everyone on campus referred to him only as 'The Admiral'. Jon had never been this close to him before and was struck speechless. The Admiral, however, did no barking or growling, just talked quietly to put him at ease.

'I have seen Professor Cherniki and he told me what happened in class. I have also listened to the taped recording of your conversation with him.'

This doubly surprised Jon; it was the first he had heard that the classes contained concealed recorders. The Admiral went on, with the very last words Jon had expected to hear.

'Congratulations, Mr Bork, you have been accepted for pilot training. Your classes begin next week – *if* you wish to continue training.' Jon started to talk, but the Admiral stopped him with an upraised palm. 'I want you to listen first before you give me your answer. As you have already discovered, space flight is not all that it appears to be.

'When we first hit space we were losing nine out of ten ships. And not through mechanical failure either. Telemetering equipment on the pilots showed us where the trouble lay –

51

space is just not made for the human body. Gravity changes, blood pressure, free fall, radiation narcosis, all of these combined with a dozen other causes we discovered later to put the pilot out of action. If he didn't black out completely or lose control, the disorientation of the new stimuli made it impossible for him to operate the ship.

'So we had a stalemate. Plenty of good ships with no one to fly them. We tried drugs, hypnosis and a number of other things to fit men for space. They all failed for the same reason. By the time we adjusted men for space they were so doped and controlled that they were again unable to do the job.

'It was Dr Moshe Kahn who solved the problem – you've heard of him?'

'Just vaguely – wasn't he first director of the Psych Corps?'

'Yes – that's all he is known for in the public record. Maybe, some day, he can get the credit due him. Dr Kahn was the man who enabled us to conquer space.

'His theory, that was proven to be absolutely true, was that man as we know him, *homo sapiens*, is unfit for space. Dr Kahn set out to create *homo nova*, men who could live and work in space. Under the correct mental conditions the human body is capable of unusual feats – such as walking through fire or possessing the rigid strength of a hypnotized patient. Dr Kahn reasoned that the body's potentialities are great enough, all he had to do was create the *mind* of *homo nova*. This he did by inducing a condition of dual personality in adults.'

'I don't understand, sir,' Jon broke in, 'wouldn't it have been easier to work with children, babies – condition them from the very beginning?'

'Of course,' the Admiral said, 'but happily we have laws to prevent just that sort of thing. Dr Kahn never considered that approach; he used men, volunteers – most of them with some experience in space. Cases of multiple personality have been documented as far back as the nineteenth century, but no one had ever tried to *create* a separate personality. Kahn did it and he created the kind of personality he wanted. What is terrifying, upsetting or uncomfortable for a normal person is the natural environment of these new personalities. They are able to pilot ships between the planets. Using frozen sleep, passengers could also be carried to the planets without experiencing the terrible rigours of space.

'The entire programme has been kept a secret – for good and obvious reasons. I can hear the howls now if people knew they were travelling with an unconscious pilot – an insane pilot I imagine they would call it since this is a kind of induced insanity. The only people who know about the programme are the instructors, the pilots and a few high officials.

'Since the pilots are all volunteers – and the programme *works* – there are no ethical rules being broken. As you have seen, even the students in this school have no idea of the real nature of a space pilot. If they accept the cover-up in their text books they go on to other jobs in the Corps. If they have the capacity to think and understand – like you – they will understand the need for a programme like this. They will have the knowledge to know what they are getting into if they volunteer.

'I think that covers the whole picture – unless you have any questions.'

Jon thought for a moment. 'Just one, and it may sound a little foolish. Just what are – the physical symptoms connected with this training? I mean will I really be a little bit—'

'Insane? Only by definition. The new personality, Jon II, can only exist in the specialized environment of the ship's control cabin. Your original personality, Jon I, assumes command all the time on the outside. The only sensation you will have will be periods of amnesia. The personalities are distinct and separate. Each blacks out completely when the other is dominant.'

Jon's mind was made up – had been made up for quite a while.

'I still look forward to being a pilot, Admiral. I don't see that all of this alters that fact any.'

They shook hands then, the Admiral a little sadly. He had done this many times before. He knew it did not always turn out exactly as the young volunteers imagined.

Jon left the school the same afternoon, without seeing any of his classmates. The Pilot Training School was in a different part of the same base and a new world altogether.

The thing he liked most was the feeling of having arrived. He was no longer treated like a student, but as a responsible equal. He was one of a select few. There were only twelve students in the school at the time and over 1,500 men on the training staff. It soon became obvious why.

The first few weeks were mostly physical examinations and tests. Then came the endless sessions with the encephalograph and in the hypno chambers. Jon had nightmares at first and many days had a period of half-awake, strange sensations. This was only in the beginning. The first step in the programme was separating the two personalities completely. Once this happened Jon I had no knowledge of Jon II. Time went by very fast for him since he wasn't aware of most of the training.

Part of the programme was orientation, teaching him how to accept and live with the hidden half of his mind. He, of course, could never meet Jon II, but he did watch another pilot's II personality. Jenkins was the one he saw, a slim boy about a year older than Jon. It was a Fine Motor Control Under Acceleration test that he watched. He found it hard to believe. The Jenkins in the test chair only faintly resembled the one he knew. Jenkins II had an expressionless face and a smoothness of motion that Jenkins I could never have. He sat in the acceleration cage that moved in sudden surges in random directions. At the same time Jenkins II had to throw small switches on a control board in response to a changing signal pattern. His fingers moved carefully, flicking the tiny switches placed only an inch apart – while the cage made sudden 3-G swoops. Jenkins II's muscles were barhard to counteract the acceleration, but it was more than mere strength that gave the control. Heightened perception noted every thrust as it started and the opposed muscles countered with exactly the right amount of counterthrust. It was the automatic balance of an old sailor on a pitching ship, refined down to the smallest motion.

When Jon II was firmly established, Jon I had some uncomfortable experiences. Instead of coming through in the psych room one day, he found himself in the hospital. There was a tremendous gash across his palm and two fingers were broken.

'Training accident,' the doctor said. 'Something went

wrong in the G cage and you saved yourself a good bit of injury by grabbing a bracing rod. Hurt your hand a little, that's all. Here's the rod.'

The doctor smiled when he gave Jon the piece of metal – and he could see why. It was half-inch steel and the weight of his body on his fingers had bent and broken the rod. Jon I would have difficulty bending it with a hammer.

All of the training was not for Jon II's benefit. Once the second personality was strongly established, training time was split about 50-50. Jon I learned everything there was to know about a spacer – outside of the control room. He took charge of the ship on the ground – check-ups, repairs, even passenger good will. Jon I was the pilot and everyone had to have faith in him. They could never know that he blacked out whenever he entered the control room.

He tried many times to see it, but never could. The control room was the deeply implanted device that triggered the personality shift. As soon as Jon I took a step through the door or even as much as glanced inside – he was through. Jon II was in his domain and took over instantly.

Graduation day was the most important, and the same time the most frustrating day of his entire life. There was no such thing as a graduating class. As each pilot finished his training he graduated at a public ceremony. Most of the base personnel turned out, at least 30,000 men. They paraded and Jon marched out in front of them in his pilot's black uniform. The Admiral himself took out the platinum wings – oldest symbol of man's flight – and snapped them on. It was a moment to remember.

There was just time to say good-bye to his family, when the ship was ready. That was another feature of graduation day. The new pilot made his first flight. A short hop to the moon with a shipload of supplies – but still a flight. He had climbed the ramp to the entrance, turned to wave to his family, small specks in the distance. Then he had stepped into the control room.

Then he had stepped out through the lock on to the surface of the moon.

There had been no sensation of time. One instant he had

55

been on Earth; in the next breath he was on the moon. Only the fact that he was wearing a spacesuit and his muscles were tired and sore convinced him. It was the most anti-climactic experience of his life. . . .

In the garden on Earth, looking up at the newly risen moon, Jon thought about the past and tasted it dry as ashes in his mouth. Inside the house someone laughed and he heard the tinkle of bottle against glass. He pushed the thoughts away then and remembered where he was.

His family's house, the party in his honour. He had put them off time after time, then was finally forced to accept. It was just as bad as he had thought it would be. It is one thing to live a lie with yourself – something totally different to be a false hero in your own home.

Squaring his shoulders and flicking a speck of invisible dust from his jacket, he went back inside.

The following morning he reported to base for the 48-hour examination and sweat period that preceded all flights. His physical system was tuned to maximum potentiality by the doctors while he was briefed on the flight. It was to be the longest yet, and the most important.

'A long trip,' the briefing officer said, tapping the chart, 'to Jupiter – or rather the eighth satellite. One of the retrograde ones. There is a base and an observatory there now, as you know, but a new bunch of observers are going out. Astrophysicists to do work with Jupiter's gravity. Twelve of them and all their equipment. That's quite a load. Your main concern – or rather II's – will be the asteroid belt. You can't get too far away from the ecliptic so you may contact meteoric debris. We've had some trouble that way already. With a little luck you should complete a successful flight.'

Jon shook hands with the passengers when they came aboard and checked the technicians when they sealed the freeze chambers. When everything was secured he climbed an internal companionway to the control room. This was the point where he always held back a bit. Once he pushed open the door he was committed. It was the last act of free will he had, then Jon II took over. He hesitated only a second, then pushed the door open, thinking to himself – *next stop, Jupiter*.

Only it wasn't Jupiter, it was pain.

He couldn't see and he couldn't hear. A thousand sensations were forced on him at once. They added up to pain. Bigger, redder and more horrifying than he ever thought possible. It took an effort of will to blink his eyes and try to focus them.

In front of him was the viewpoint and beyond it was the stars. He was in space, in the cabin of the ship. For an instant he almost forgot the pain at the sight of the stars spread out before him. Then the pain was back and he was trying to understand what had happened, wanting to do something to end the torment. The cabin was dark, the only illumination the lights on the giant control boards. They flickered and changed, he had no idea of their meaning or what to do.

Then the pain was too much and he screamed and lost consciousness.

In the few moments Jon I had been in command of their body, Jon II had drained away a little of his panic. He had lost control and blacked out. He couldn't let it happen again. Neural blocks cut off a good deal of the pain, but enough seeped through to interfere with his thinking. A meteorite – it must have been a meteorite.

There was a fist-sized opening in the front bulkhead, and flair was roaring out through the gap. He could see a single star through the hole, brighter and clearer than any star he had ever seen before. The meteorite had made that hole, then hit the wall behind him. That must have been the explosion and the glare when it vapourized. It had done a lot of damage, sprayed molten metal all over him and destroyed the circuits in his chair pedestal. It was getting hard to breathe, the air was almost gone. And cold.

The spacesuit was in its locker, just ten feet away. Only the straps that held him in the chair couldn't be opened. The electric release was destroyed, the mechanical release jammed. He struggled with the clasps, but he only had his bare hands.

All the time it was getting harder to breathe. The panic was there again and he could no longer fight it away.

Jon II gasped and his eyes closed. Jon I opened them.

The pain was overwhelming and washed over him instantly. Jon's eyes closed again and his body slumped forward.

Then he straightened and jerkily the eyelids opened. For a moment his eyeballs rolled unsteadily, then fixed. They looked straight ahead and were almost vacant of anything like reason.

For Jon III was closer to the basic animal than any man or animal that had ever walked the earth. *Survive* was the only thing he knew. *Survive* and *save the ship*. He was dimly aware of Jon I and Jon II and could call on their memories if he needed to. He had no memories or thoughts of his own – except pain. Born in pain and doomed forever to live in pain, his whole world was pain.

Jon III was a built-in safety device, an admission that there might be times when even the II personality of a pilot couldn't save the ship. Only in the last extreme, when all else had failed, could the III personality assume control.

There was nothing at all subtle about Jon III's control. *See a problem – solve the problem*. The memory, still in his forebrain, was 'get the spacesuit'. He started to stand up, then realized for the first time he couldn't. With both hands he pulled against the strap across his chest, but it didn't break. The clasp was the answer; he had to open that.

No tools, just his hands. Use his hands. He put one finger inside the clasp and pulled. The finger bent, stretched and broke. Jon III felt no pain at all, no emotion. He put his second finger in and tugged again. The second finger was almost pulled off, and hung only by a piece of flesh. He put in the third finger.

The clasp finally broke when he pulled with his thumb. The rest of the hand hung, broken and disfigured. With a surge of power he pushed himself out of the chair. The femur in his right leg cracked and broke at the same time the lower strap did. Pulling with his good hand and pushing with his left leg he squirmed across the floor to the spacesuit cabinet.

The air in the cabin was almost a vacuum. He had to keep blinking to wash away the ice crystals that formed on his eyes. His heart was beating at four times its regular rate to force the trace of oxygen to the dying body.

Jon III was aware of these things, but they didn't bother him. His world had always been like that. The only way he could regain the peace of his mindless oblivion was to finish what he had started. He never knew, had never been taught, that dying was also a way out.

Carefully and methodically he pulled down the spacesuit and climbed into it. He turned the oxygen on and closed the last zipper. Then he closed his eyes with a sigh of relief.

Jon II opened his eyes and felt the pain. He could bear it now because he knew he was going to get out of this mess and save the ship. An emergency patch stopped the rush of air and while pressure was building up from the reserve tanks he examined the board. The ship could be flown on the secondary and manual circuits. All he had to do was rig them.

When the pressure reached seven pounds he stripped off the spacesuit and gave himself first-aid. He was a little surprised to see the state his right hand was in. He couldn't remember doing that. Jon II wasn't equipped to solve that kind of problem though. He hurried the dressings and burn ointment and turned back to his repairs. It was going to be a successful trip after all.

Jon never knew about Jon III – he was the unknown safety factor that was there always, dormant and waiting. Jon I thought Jon II had got them out of the mess. Jon II didn't bother to think about things like that. His job was to fly the ship.

Jon recuperated slowly at the hospital on Jupiter 8. He was amazed at the amount of damage his body had suffered, yet pulled through. The pain was bad for a long time, but he didn't really mind. It wasn't too high a price to pay.

He wasn't going to be a liar any more. He had been a pilot, even if for only a few seconds.

He had seen the stars in space.

FINAL ENCOUNTER

I

Hautamaki had landed the ship on a rubble-covered pan of rock, a scored and ancient lava flow on the wrong side of the glacier. Tjond had thought, but only to herself, that they could have landed nearer; but Hautamaki was shipmaster and made all the decisions. Then again, she could have stayed with the ship. No one had forced her to join in this hideous scramble across the fissured ice. But of course staying behind was out of the question.

There was a radio beacon of some kind over there – on this uninhabited planet – sending out squeals and cracklings on a dozen frequencies. She *had* to be there when they found it.

Gulyas helped her over a difficult place and she rewarded him with a quick kiss on his windburned cheek.

It was too much to hope that it could be anything other than a human beacon, though their ship was supposed to be covering an unexplored area. Yet there was the slimmest chance that some *others* might have built the beacon. The thought of not being there at the time of a discovery like that was unbearable. How long had mankind been looking now, for how many time-dimmed centuries?

She had to rest, she was not used to this kind of physical effort. She was roped between the two men and when she stopped they all stopped. Hautamaki halted and looked when he felt her hesitant tug on the rope, staring down at her and saying nothing. His body said it for him, arrogant, tall, heavily muscled, bronzed and nude under the transparent atmosphere suit. He was breathing lightly and normally, and his face never changed expression as he looked at her desperately heaving breast. Hautamaki! What kind of a man are you, Hautamaki, to ignore a woman with such a deadly glance?

For Hautamaki it had been the hardest thing he had ever done. When the two strangers had walked up the extended tongue of the ship's boarding ramp he had felt violated.

This was his ship, his and Kiiskinen's. But Kiiskinen was dead and the child that they had wanted to have was dead. Dead before birth, before conception. Dead because Kiiskinen was gone and Hautamaki would never want a child again. Yet there was still the job to be done; they had completed barely half of their survey swing when the accident had occurred. To return to survey base would have been prodigiously wasteful of fuel and time, so he had called for instructions – and this had been the result. A new survey team, unfledged and raw.

They had been awaiting first assignment – which meant they at least had the training if not the experience. Physically they would do the work that needed to be done. There would be no worry about that. But they were a team, and he was only half a team; and loneliness can be a terrible thing.

He would have welcomed them if Kiiskinen had been there. Now he loathed them.

The man came first, extending his hand. 'I'm Gulyas, as you know, and my wife Tjond.' He nodded over his shoulder and smiled, the hand still out.

'Welcome aboard my ship,' Hautamaki said and clasped his own hands behind his back. If this fool didn't know about the social customs of Men, he was not going to teach him.

'Sorry. I forgot you don't shake hands or touch strangers.' Still smiling, Gulyas moved aside to make room for his wife to enter the ship.

'How do you do, shipmaster?' Tjond said. Then her eyes widened and she flushed, as she saw for the first time that he was completely nude.

'I'll show you your quarters,' Hautamaki said, turning and walking away, knowing they would follow. A woman! He had seen them before on various planets, even talked with them, but never had he believed that there would some day be one on his ship. How ugly they were, with their swollen bodies! It was no wonder that on the other worlds everyone wore clothes, to conceal those blubbery, bobbing things and the excess fat below.

61

'Why – he wasn't even wearing *shoes*!' Tjond said indignantly as she closed the door. Gulyas laughed.

'Since when has nudity bothered you? You didn't seem to mind it during our holiday on Hie. And you knew about the Men's customs.'

'That was different. Everyone was dressed – or undressed – the same. But this, it's almost indecent!'

'One man's indecency is another's decency.'

'I bet you can't say that three times fast.'

'Nevertheless it's true. When you come down to it he probably thinks that we're just as socially wrong as you seem to think he is.'

'I don't think – I *know*!' she said, reaching up on tiptoes to nip his ear with her tiny teeth, as white and perfectly shaped as rice grains. 'How long have we been married?'

'Six days, nineteen hours standard, and some odd minutes.'

'Only odd because you haven't kissed me in such a terribly long time.'

He smiled down at her tiny, lovely figure, ran his hand over the warm firmness of her hairless skull and down her straight body, brushing the upturned almost vestigial buds of her breasts.

'You're beautiful,' he said, then kissed her.

II

Once they were across the glacier the going was easier on the hard-packed snow. Within an hour they had reached the base of the rocky spire. It stretched above them against the green-tinted sky, black and fissured. Tjond let her eyes travel up its length and wanted to cry.

'It's too tall! *Impossible* to climb. With the gravsled we could ride up.'

'We have discussed this before,' Hautamaki said, looking at Gulyas as he always did when he talked to her. 'I will bring no radiation sources near the device up there until we determine what it is. Nothing can be learned from our aerial photograph except that it appears to be an untended machine of some kind.

I will climb first. You may follow. It is not difficult on this type of rock.'

It was not difficult – it was downright impossible. She scrambled and fell and couldn't get a body's-length up the spire. In the end she untied her rope. As soon as the two men had climbed above her she sobbed hopelessly into her hands. Gulyas must have heard her, or he knew how she felt being left out, because he called back down to her.

'I'll drop you a rope as soon as we get to the top, with a loop on the end. Slip your arms through it, and I'll pull you up.'

She was sure that he wouldn't be able to do it, but still she had to try. The beacon – it might *not* be human made!

The rope cut into her body, and surprisingly enough he could pull her up. She did her best to keep from banging into the cliff and twisting about: then Gulyas was reaching down to help her. Hautamaki was holding the rope . . . and she knew that it was the strength of those corded arms, not her husband's, that had brought her so quickly up.

'Hautamaki, thank you for—'

'We will examine the device now,' he said, interrupting her and looking at Gulyas while he spoke. 'You will both stay here with my pack. Do not approach unless you are ordered to.'

He turned on his heel, and with purposeful stride went to the outcropping where the machine stood. No more than a pace away from it he dropped to one knee, his body hiding most of it from sight, staying during long minutes in this cramped position.

'What is he doing?' Tjond whispered, hugging tight to Gulyas' arm. 'What is it? What does he see?'

'Come over here!' Hautamaki said, standing. There was a ring of emotion in his voice that they had never heard before. They ran, skidding on the ice-glazed rock, stopping only at the barrier of his outstretched arm.

'What do you make of it?' Hautamaki asked, never taking his eyes from the squat machine fixed to the rock before them.

There was a central structure, a half sphere of yellowish metal that clamped tight to the rock, its bottom edge conforming to the irregularities beneath it. From this projected stubby arms of the same material, arranged around the circumference close to the base. On each arm was a shorter length of metal. Each one was shaped differently, but all were pointing sky-wards like questing fingers. An arm-thick cable emerged from the side of the hemisphere and crawled over to a higher shelf of rock. There it suddenly straightened and stood straight up, rearing into the air above their heads. Gulyas pointed to this.

'I have no idea what the other parts do, but I'll wager that is the antenna that has been sending out the signals we picked up when we entered this system.'

'It might be,' Hautamaki admitted. 'But what about the rest?'

'One of those things that's pointing up towards the sky looks like a little telescope,' Tjond said. 'I really believe it is.'

Hautamaki gave an angry cry and reached for her as she knelt on the ground, but he was too late. She pressed one eye to the bottom of the tube, squinted the other shut and tried to see.

'Why – yes, it is a telescope!' She opened the other eye and examined the sky. 'I can see the edge of the clouds up there very clearly.'

Gulyas pulled her away, but there was no danger. It was a telescope, as she had said, nothing more. They took turns looking through it. It was Hautamaki who noticed that it was slowly moving.

'In that case – all of the others must be turning too, since they are parallel,' Gulyas said, pointing to the metal devices that tipped each arm. One of them had an eyepiece not unlike the telescope's, but when he looked into it there was only darkness. 'I can't see a thing through it,' he said.

'Perhaps *you* weren't intended to,' Hautamaki said, rubbing his jaw while he stared at the strange machine, then turned away to rummage in his pack. He took a multi-radiation tester from its padded carrying case and held it before the eyepiece that Gulyas had been trying to look through. 'Infra-red radiation only. Everything else is screened out.'

Another of the tube-like things appeared to focus ultra-violet rays, while an open latticework of metal plates concentrated radio waves. It was Tjond who voiced the thought they all had.

64

'If I looked through a telescope – perhaps all these other things are telescopes too! Only made for alien eyes, as if the creatures who built the thing didn't know who, or what, would be coming here and provided all kinds of telescopes working on all kinds of wavelengths. The search is over! We . . . mankind . . . we're not alone in the universe after all!'

'We mustn't leap to conclusions,' Hautamaki said, but the tone of his voice belied his words.

'Why not?' Gulyas shouted, hugging his wife to him in a spasm of emotion. 'Why shouldn't we be the ones to find the aliens? If they exist at all we knew we would come across them some time! The galaxy is immense – but finite. *Look and you shall find*. Isn't that what it says over the entrance to the academy?'

'We have no real evidence yet,' Hautamaki said, trying not to let his own growing enthusiasm show. He was the leader, he must be the devil's advocate. 'This device could have been human made.'

'Point one,' Gulyas said, ticking off on his finger. 'It resembles nothing that any of us have ever seen before. Secondly, it is made of a tough unknown alloy. And thirdly it is in a section of space that, as far as we know, has never been visited before. We are light-centuries from the nearest inhabited system, and ships that can make this sort of trip and return are only a relatively recent development. . . .'

'And here is *real* evidence – without any guesswork!' Tjond shouted, and they ran over to her.

She had followed the heavy cable that transformed itself into the aerial. At the base, where it was thickened and fastened to the rock, were a series of incised characters. There must have been hundreds of them, rising from ground level to above their heads, each one clear and distinct.

'Those aren't human,' Tjond said triumphantly. 'They do not bear the slightest resemblance to any written characters of any language known to man. They are *new*!'

'How can you be sure?' Hautamaki said, forgetting himself enough to address her directly.

'I know, shipmaster, because this is my specialty. I trained in

65

comparative philology and specialized in abbicciology – the study of the history of alphabets. We are probably the only science that is in touch with earth—'

'Impossible!'

'No, just very slow. Earth must be halfway around the galaxy from where we are now. If I remember correctly, it takes about four hundred years for a round-trip communication. Abbicciology is a study that can only grow at the outer fringes; we deal with a hard core of unalterable fact. The old Earth alphabets are part of history and cannot be changed. I have studied them all, every character and every detail, and I have observed their mutations through the millennia. It can be observed that no matter how alphabets are modified and changed they will retain elements of their progenitors. That is the letter "L" as it has been adapted for computer input.' She scratched it into the rock with the tip of her knife, then incised a wavy character next to it. 'And this is the Hebrew *lamedh*, in which you can see the same basic shape. Hebrew is a proto-alphabet, so ancient as to be almost unbelievable. Yet there is the same right-angle bend. But these characters – there is *nothing* there that I have ever seen before.'

The silence stretched on while Hautamaki looked at her, studied her as if the truth or falsity of her words might be written somehow on her face. Then he smiled.

'I'll take your word for it. I'm sure you know your field very well.' He walked back to his pack and began taking out more test instruments.

'Did you see that,' Tjond whispered in her husband's ear, 'he *smiled* at me.'

'Nonsense. It is probably the first rictus of advanced frostbite.'

Hautamaki had hung a weight from the barrel of the telescope and was timing its motion over the ground. 'Gulyas,' he asked, 'do you remember this planet's period of rotation?'

'Roughly eighteen standard hours. The computation wasn't exact. Why?'

'That's close enough. We are at about 85 degrees north latitude here, which conforms to the angle of those rigid arms, while the motion of these scopes . . .'

'Counteracts the planet's rotation, moving at the same speed in the opposite direction. Of course! I should have seen it.'

'What are you two talking about?' Tjond asked.

'They all point to the same spot in the sky all the time,' Gulyas said. 'To a star.'

'It could be another planet in this system,' Hautamaki said, then shook his head. 'No, there is no reason for that. It is something outside. We will tell after dark.'

They were comfortable in their atmosphere suits and had enough food and water. The machine was photographed and studied from every angle and they theorized on its possible power source. In spite of this the hours dragged by until dusk. There were some clouds, but they cleared away before sunset. When the first star appeared in the darkening sky Hautamaki bent to the ocular of the telescope.

'Just sky. Too light yet. But there is some sort of glowing grid appearing in the field, five thin lines radiating in from the circumference. Instead of crossing they fade as they come to the centre.'

'But they'll point out whatever star is in the centre of the field – without obscuring it?'

'Yes. The stars are appearing now.'

It was a seventh-magnitude star, isolated near the galactic rim. It appeared commonplace in every way except for its location with no nearby neighbours even in stellar terms. They took turns looking at it, marking it so they could not possibly mistake it for any other.

'Are we going there?' Tjond asked, though it was more of a statement than a question that sought an answer.

'Of course,' Hautamaki said.

III

As soon as their ship had cleared atmosphere, Hautamaki sent a message to the nearest relay station. While they waited for an answer they analysed the material they had.

With each result their enthusiasm grew. The metal was no

harder than some of the resistant alloys they used, but its composition was completely different and some unknown process of fabrication had been used that had compacted the surface molecules to a greater density. The characters bore no resemblance to any human alphabet. And the star towards which the instruments had been pointed was far beyond the limits of galactic exploration.

When the message arrived, *signal recorded*, they jumped the ship at once on the carefully computed and waiting course. Their standing instructions were to investigate anything, report everything, and this they were doing. With their planned movements recorded they were free. They, *they*, were going to make a first contact with an alien race – had already made contact with one of its artifacts. No matter what happened now, the honour was irrevocably theirs. The next meal turned naturally into a celebration, and Hautamaki unbent enough to allow other intoxicants as well as wine. The results were almost disastrous.

'A toast!' Tjond shouted, standing and wobbling just a bit.

'To Earth and mankind – no longer alone!'

No longer alone, they repeated, and Hautamaki's face lost some of the party gaiety that it had reluctantly gained.

'I ask you to join me in a toast,' he said, 'to someone you never knew, who should have been here to share this with us.'

'To Kiiskinen,' Gulyas said. He had read the records and knew about the tragedy that was still fresh in Hautamaki's thoughts.

'Thank you. To Kiiskinen.' They drank.

'I wish we could have met him,' Tjond said, a tendril of feminine curiosity tickling at her.

'A fine man,' Hautamaki said, seeming anxious to talk now that the subject had been broached for the first time since the accident. 'One of the very finest. We were twelve years on this ship.'

'Did you have . . . children?' Tjond asked.

'Your curiosity is not fitting,' Gulyas snapped at his wife. 'I think it would be better if we dropped . . .'

Hautamaki held up his hand. 'Please. I understand your

natural interest. We Men have settled only a dozen or so planets and I imagine our customs are curious to you; we are only in a minority as yet. But if there is any embarrassment it is all your own. Are you embarrassed about being bisexual? Would you kiss your wife in public?'

'A pleasure,' Gulyas said, and did.

'Then you understand what I mean. We feel the same way and at times act the same way, though our society is mono-sexual. It was a natural result of ectogenesis.'

'Not natural,' Tjond said, a touch of colour in her cheeks. 'Ectogenesis needs a fertile ovum. Ova comes from females; an ectogenetic society should logically be a female society. An all-male one is unnatural.'

'Everything we do is unnatural,' Hautamaki told her with-out apparent anger. 'Man is an environment-changing animal. Every person living away from Earth is living in an "un-natural" environment. Ectogenesis on these terms is no more unnatural than living, as we are now, in a metal hull in an un-real manifestation of space-time. That this ectogenesis should combine the germ plasm from two male cells rather than from an egg and a sperm is of no more relevancy than your vestigial breasts.'

'You are being insulting,' she said, blushing.

'Not in the least. They have lost their function, therefore they are degenerative. You bisexuals are just as natural – or unnatural – as we Men. Neither is viable without the "un-natural" environment that we have created.'

The excitement of their recent discovery still possessed them, and perhaps the stimulants and the anger had lowered Tjond's control. 'Why – how dare you call me unnatural – you—'

'You forget yourself, woman!' Hautamaki boomed, drown-ing out the word, leaping to his feet. 'You expected to pry into the intimate details of my life and are insulted when I mention some of your own taboos. The Men are better off without your kind!' He drew a deep, shuddering breath, turned on his heel and left the room.

Tjond stayed in their quarters for almost a standard week after that evening. She worked on her analysis of the alien characters and Gulyas brought her meals. Hautamaki did not mention the events, and cut Gulyas off when he tried to apologize for his wife. But he made no protest when she appeared again in the control section, though he reverted to his earlier custom of speaking only to Gulyas, never addressing her directly.

'Did he actually want me to come too?' Tjond asked, closing her tweezers on a single tiny hair that marred the ivory sweep of her smooth forehead and skull. She pulled it out and touched her brow. 'Have you noticed that he really has eyebrows? Right *here*, great shabby things like an atavism. Even hair around the base of his skull. Disgusting. I'll bet you that the Men sort their genes for hirsuteness, it couldn't be accident. You never answered – did he ask for me to be there?'

'You never gave me a chance to answer,' Gulyas told her, a smile softening his words. 'He didn't ask for you by name. That would be expecting too much. But he did say that there would be a full crew meeting at nineteen hours.'

She put a touch of pink make-up on the lobes of her ears and the bottoms of her nostrils, then snapped her cosmetic case shut. 'I'm ready whenever you are. Shall we go see what the shipmaster wants?'

'In twenty hours we'll be breaking out of jump-space,' Hautamaki told them when they had met in the control section. 'There is a very good chance that we will encounter the people – the aliens – who constructed the beacon. Until we discover differently we will assume that they are peacefully inclined. Yes, Gulyas?'

'Shipmaster, there has been a good deal of controversy on the intentions of any hypothetical race that might be encountered. There has been no real agreement . . .'

'It does not matter. I am shipmaster. The evidence so far indicates a race looking for contact, not conquest. I see it this way. We have a rich and very old culture, so while we have been searching for another intelligent life form we have also been exploring and recording with ships like this one. A poorer culture might be limited in the number of ships that they could apply to this kind of occupation. Therefore the beacons.

Many of them could be easily planted by a single ship over a large area of space. There are undoubtedly others. All of them serve to draw attention to a single star, a rendezvous point of some type.'

'This doesn't prove peaceful intentions. It could be a trap.'

'I doubt it. There are far better ways to satisfy warlike tendencies than to set elaborate traps like this. I *think* their intentions are peaceful, and that is the only factor that matters. Until we actually encounter them any action will have to be based on a guess. Therefore I have already jettisoned the ship's armament—'

'You *what?*'

' – and I'll ask you to surrender any personal weapons that you might have in your possession.'

'You're risking our lives – without even consulting us,' Tjond said angrily.

'Not at all,' he answered, not looking at her. 'You risked your own life when you entered the service and took the oath. You will obey my instructions. All weapons here within the hour; I want the ship clean before we break through. We will meet the strangers armed only with our humanity. . . . You may think the Men go naked for some perverse reason, but that is wrong. We have discarded clothes as detrimental to total involvement in our environment, a both practical and symbolic action.'

'You aren't suggesting that *we* remove our clothes as well, are you?' Tjond asked, still angry.

'Not at all. Do as you please. I am just attempting to explain my reasons so we will have some unanimity of action when we encounter the intelligent creatures who built the beacon. Survey knows now where we are. If we do not return, a later contact team will be protected by mankind's complete armoury of death. So we will now give our aliens every opportunity to kill us – if that is what they are planning. Retribution will follow. If they do not have warlike intentions we will make peaceful contact. That, in itself, is reason enough to risk one's life a hundred times over. I don't have to explain to you the monumental importance of such a contact.'

The tension grew as the time for break-through approached. The box of handguns, explosive charges, poisons from the laboratory – even the large knives from the kitchen – had long since been jettisoned. They were all in the control area when the bell pinged softly and they broke through, back into normal space. Here, at the galactic rim, most of the stars were massed to one side. Ahead lay a pit of blackness with a single star glowing.

'That's it,' Gulyas said, swinging back the spectral analyser, 'but we're not close enough for clear observation. Are we going to take another jump now?'

'No,' Hautamaki said. 'I want a clevs observation first.'

The sensitive clevs screen began to glow as soon as the pressure dropped, darkening slowly. There were occasional bursts of light from their surface as random molecules of air struck them, then this died away. The forward screen deepened to the blackness of outer space and in its centre appeared the image of the star.

'It's impossible!' Tjond gasped from the observer's seat behind them.

'Not impossible,' Hautamaki said. 'Just impossible of natural origin. Its existence proves that what we see can – and has – been constructed. We will proceed.'

The star image burned with unreality. The star itself at the core was normal enough – but how to explain the three interlocking rings that circled it? They had the dimensions of a planetary orbit. Even if they were as tenuous as a comet's tail their construction was an incredible achievement. And what could be the significance of the coloured lights on the rings, apparently orbiting the primary like insane electrons?

The screen sparkled and the image faded.

'It could only be a beacon,' Hautamaki said, removing his helmet. 'It is there to draw attention, as was the radio beacon that drew us to the last planet. What race with the curiosity to build spaceships could possibly resist the attraction of a thing like that?'

Gulyas was feeding the course corrections into the computor. 'It is still baffling,' he said. 'With the physical ability to construct that why haven't they built an exploring fleet to go out and make contacts – instead of trying to draw them in?'

'I hope that we will discover that answer soon. Though it probably lies in whatever composes their alien psychology. To their way of thinking this might be the obvious manner. And you will have to admit that it has worked.'

IV

This time when they made the transition from jumpspace the glowing rings of light filled the front ports. Their radio receivers were on, automatically searching the wavelengths.

They burst into sound on a number of bands simultaneously. Gulyas lowered the volume.

'This is the same kind of broadcast we had from the beacon,' he said. 'Very directional. All of the transmissions are coming from that golden planetoid, or whatever it is. It's big, but doesn't seem to have a planetary diameter.'

'We're on our way,' Hautamaki told him. 'I'll take the controls, see if you can get any image on the video circuits.'

'Just interference. But I'm sending out a signal, a view of this cabin. If they have the right equipment there they should be able to analyse our signal and match it. . . . Look, the screen is changing! They're working fast.'

The viewscreen was rippling with colour. Then a picture appeared, blurred, then steadied. Tjond focused and it snapped into clear life. The two men looked, stared. Behind them Tjond gasped.

'At least no snakes or insects, praise fortune for that!'

The being on the screen was staring at them with the same intensity. There was no way to estimate its relative size, but it was surely humanoid. Three long fingers, heavily webbed, with an opposed thumb. Only the upper part of its figure was visible, and this was clothed so that no physical details could be seen. But the being's face stood out clearly on the screen, golden in colour, hairless, with large, almost circular eyes. Its nose, had it been a human one, would be said to be broken, spread over its face, nostrils flaring. This, and the cleft upper lip, gave it a grim appearance to human eyes.

But this yardstick could not be applied. By alien standards it might be beautiful.

'S'bb'thik,' the creature said. The radio beacons carried the matching audio now. The voice was high-pitched and squeaky.

'I greet you as well,' Hautamaki said. 'We both have spoken languages and we will learn to understand each other. But we come in peace.'

'Maybe we do, but I can't say the same thing for these aliens,' Gulyas interrupted. 'Look at screen three.'

This held an enlarged view taken from one of the forward pickups, locked onto the planetoid they were approaching. A group of dark buildings stood out from the golden surface, crowned with a forest of aerials and antennas. Ringed about the building were circular structures mounted with squat tubular devices that resembled heavy-bore weapons. The similarity was increased by the fact that the numerous emplacements had rotated. The open orifices were tracking the approaching ship.

'I'm killing our approach velocity,' Hautamaki said, stabbing the control buttons in rapid sequence. 'Set up a repeater plate here and switch on a magnified view of those weapons. We'll find out their intentions right now.'

Once their motion relative to the golden planetoid had been stopped, Hautamaki turned and pointed to the repeater screen, slowly tapping the image of the weapons. Then he tapped himself on the chest and raised his hands before him, fingers spread wide, empty. The alien had watched this dumb show with glistening, golden eyes. It rocked its head from side to side and repeated Hautamaki's gesture, tapping itself on the chest with its long central finger, then pointed into the screen.

'He understood at once,' Gulyas said. 'Those weapons – they're turning away, sinking out of sight.'

'We'll continue our approach. Are you recording this?'

'Sight, sound, full readings from every instrument. We've been recording since we first saw the star, with the tapes being fed into the armoured vault as you ordered. I wonder what the next step is?'

'They've already taken it – look.'

The image of the alien reached off the screen and brought back what appeared to be a metal sphere that it held lightly in one hand. From the sphere projected a pipe-like extrusion of metal with a lever half way up its length. When the alien pressed the lever they heard a hissing.

'A tank of gas,' Gulyas said. 'I wonder what it is supposed to signify? No – it's not gas. It must be a vacuum. See, the pipe is sucking up those grains sprinkled on the table.' The alien kept the lever depressed until the hissing stopped.

'Ingenious,' Hautamaki said. 'Now we know there is a sample of their atmosphere inside that tank.'

There was no mechanical propulsion visible, but the sphere came swooping up towards their ship where it swung in orbit above the golden planetoid. The sphere stopped, just outside the ship and clearly visible from the viewports, bobbing in a small arc.

'Some sort of force beam,' Hautamaki said, 'though nothing registers on the hull instruments. That's one thing I hope we find out how to do. I'm going to open the outer door on the main hatch.'

As soon as the door opened the sphere swooped and vanished from sight and they saw, through the pickup inside the air lock, that it fell gently to the deck inside. Hautamaki closed the door and pointed to Gulyas.

'Take a pair of insulated gloves and carry that tank to the lab. Run the contents through the usual air examination procedures that we use for testing planetary atmosphere. As soon as you have taken the sample evacuate the tank and fill it with our own air, then throw it out through the lock.'

The analysers worked on the sample of alien air, and presumably the aliens were doing the same with their tank of ship's atmosphere. The analysis was routine and fast, the report appearing in coded form on the panel in control.

'Unbreathable,' Gulyas said, 'at least for us. There seems to be enough oxygen, more than enough, but any of those sulphurated compounds would eat holes through our lungs. They must have rugged metabolisms to inhale stuff like that. One thing is certain, we'll never be in competition for the same worlds. . . .'

'Look! The picture is changing,' Tjond said, drawing their attention back to the viewing screen.

The alien had vanished and the viewpoint appeared to be in space above the planetoid's surface. A transparent bulge on its surface filled the screen, and while they watched, the alien entered it from below. The scene shifted again, then they were looking at the alien from inside the clear-walled chamber. The alien came towards the pickup, but before reaching it the alien stopped and leaned against what appeared to be thin air.

'There's a transparent wall that divided the dome in half,' Gulyas said. 'I'm beginning to get the idea.'

The pickup panned away from the alien, swept around to the opposite direction where there was an entrance cut into the clear fabric of the wall. The door was open into space.

'That's obvious enough,' Hautamaki said, rising to his feet. 'That central wall must be airtight, so it can be used for a conference chamber. I'll go. Keep a record of everything.'

'It looks like a trap,' Tjond said, fidgeting with her fingers while she looked at the invitingly open door on the screen. 'It will be a risk. . . .'

Hautamaki laughed, the first time they had ever heard him do so, as he climbed into his pressure suit. 'A trap! Do you believe they have gone to all this to set a trap for me? Such ego is preposterous. And if it were a trap – do you think it possible to stay out of it?'

He pushed himself free of the ship. His suited figure floated away, getting smaller and smaller.

Silently, moving closer together without realizing they did so, they watched the meeting on the screen. They saw Hautamaki drawn gently in through the open doorway until his feet touched the floor. He turned to look as the door closed, while from the radio they heard a hissing, very dimly at first, then louder and louder.

'It sounds like they are pressurizing the room,' Gulyas said.

Hautamaki nodded. "Yes, I can hear it now, and there is a reading on the external pressure gauge. As soon as it reaches atmospheric normal I'm taking my helmet off.'

Tjond started to protest, but stopped when her husband raised his hand in warning. This was Hautamaki's decision to make.

'Smells perfectly breathable,' Hautamaki said, 'though it has a metallic odour.'

He laid his helmet aside and stripped his suit off. The alien was standing at the partition and Hautamaki walked over until they stood face to face, almost the same height. The alien placed his palm flat against the transparent wall and the human put his hand over the same spot. They met, as close as they could, separated only by a centimetre of substance. Their eyes joined and they stared for a long time, trying to read intent, trying to communicate. The alien turned away first, walking over to a table littered with a variety of objects. It picked up the nearest one and held it for Hautamaki to see. '*Kilt*,' the alien said. It looked like a piece of stone.

Hautamaki for the first time took notice of the table on his side of the partition. It appeared to hold the identical objects as the other table, and the first of these was a lump of ordinary stone. He picked it up.

'Stone,' he said, then turned to the television pickup and the unseen viewers in the ship. 'It appears that a language lesson is first. This is obvious. See that this is recorded separately. Then we can programme the computor for machine translation in case the aliens aren't doing it themselves.'

The language lesson progressed slowly once the stock of simple nouns with physical referents had been exhausted. Films were shown, obviously prepared long before, showing simple actions and, bit by bit, verbs and tense were exchanged. The alien made no attempt to learn their language, he just worked to insure accuracy of identity in the words. They were recording too. As the language lesson progressed Gulyas's frown deepened, and he started to make notes, then a list that he checked off. Finally he interrupted the lesson.

'Hautamaki – this is important. Find out if they are just accumulating a vocabulary or if they are feeding a MT with this material.'

The answer came from the alien itself. It turned its head sideways, as if listening to a distant voice, then spoke into a cup-like device at the end of a wire. A moment later Hautamaki's voice spoke out, toneless since each word had been recorded separately.

'I talk through a machine . . . I talk my talk . . . a machine talk your talk to you . . . I am Liem . . . we need have more words in machine before talk well.'

'This can't wait,' Gulyas said. 'Tell them that we want a sample of some of their body cells, any cells at all. It is complex, but try to get it across.'

The aliens were agreeable. They did not insist on a specimen in return, but accepted one. A sealed container brought a frozen sliver of what looked like muscle tissue over to the ship. Gulyas started towards the lab.

'Take care of the recordings,' he told his wife. 'I don't think this will take too long.'

V

It didn't. Within the hour he had returned, coming up so silently that Tjond, intent on listening to the language lesson, did not notice him until he stood next to her.

'Your face,' she said. 'What is wrong? What did you discover?'

He smiled dryly to her. 'Nothing terrible, I assure you. But things are very different from what we supposed.'

'What is it?' Hautamaki asked from the screen. He had heard their voices and turned towards the pickup.

'How has the language progressed?' Gulyas asked. 'Can you understand me, Liem?'

'Yes,' the alien said. 'Almost all of the words are clear now. But the machine has only a working force of a few thousand words so you must keep your speech simple.'

'I understand. The things I want to say are very simple. First a question. Your people, do they come from a planet orbiting about a star near here?'

'No. We have travelled a long way to this star, searching. My home world is there, among those stars there.'

'Do all your people live on that world?'

'No, we live on many worlds, but we are all children of children of children of people who lived on one world very long ago.'

'Our people have also settled many worlds, but we all come

from one world,' Gulyas told him, then looked down at the paper in his hands. He smiled at the alien in the screen before him, but there was something terribly sad about this smile. 'We came originally from a planet named Earth. That is where your people came from too. We are brothers, Liem.'

'What madness is this?' Hautamaki shouted at him, his face swollen and angry. 'Liem is humanoid, not human! It cannot breathe our air!'

'*He* cannot breath our air, or perhaps she,' Gulyas answered quietly. 'We do not use gene manipulation, but we know that it is possible. I'm sure we will eventually discover just how Liem's people were altered to live under the physical conditions they do now. It might have been natural selection and normal mutation, but it seems too drastic a change to be explained that way. But that is not important. *This* is.' He held up the sheets of notes and photographs. 'You can see for yourself. This is the DNR chain from the nucleus of one of my own cells. This is Liem's. They are identical. His people are as human as we are.'

'They can't be!' Tjond shook her head in bewilderment. 'Just look at him, he is so different, and their alphabet – what about that? I cannot be wrong about that.'

'There is one possibility you did not allow for, a totally independent alphabet. You yourself told me that there is not the slightest similarity between the Chinese ideographs and western letters. If Liem's people suffered a cultural disaster that forced them to completely reinvent writing you would have your alien alphabet. As to the way they look – just consider the thousands of centuries that have passed since mankind left Earth and you will see that his physical differences are minor. Some are natural and some may have been artifically achieved, but germ plasm cannot lie. We are all the sons of man.'

'It is possible,' Liem said, speaking for the first time. 'I am informed that our biologists agree with you. Our points of difference are minor when compared to the points of similarity. Where is this Earth you come from?'

Hautamaki pointed at the sky above them, at the star-filled sweep of the Milky Way, burning with massed stars. 'There, far out there on the other side of the core, roughly half way around the lens of the galaxy.'

'The core explains partially what must have happened,' Gulyas said. 'It is thousands of light-years in diameter and over 10,000 degrees in temperature. We have explored its fringes. No ship could penetrate it or even approach too closely because of the dust clouds that surround it. So we have expanded outwards, slowly circling the rim of the galaxy, moving away from Earth. If we stopped to think about it we should have realized that mankind was moving the other way, too, in the opposite direction around the wheel.'

'And sometime we would have to meet,' Liem said. 'Now I greet you, brothers. And I am sad, because I know what this means.'

'We are alone,' Hautamaki said, looking at the massed trillions of stars. 'We have closed the circle and found only ourselves. The galaxy is ours, but we are alone.' He turned about, not realizing that Liem, the golden alien – the man – had turned at the same time in the same manner.

They faced outwards, looking at the infinite depth and infinite blackness of intergalactic space, empty of stars. Dimly, distantly, there were spots of light, microscopic blurs against the darkness, not stars but island universes, like the one at whose perimeter they stood.

These two beings were different in many ways: in the air they breathed, the colour of their skins, their languages, mannerisms, cultures. They were as different as the day is from the night: the flexible fabric of mankind had been warped by the countless centuries until they could no longer recognize each other. But time, distance and mutation could not change one thing; they were still men, still human.

'It is certain then,' Hautamaki said, 'we are alone in the galaxy.'

'Alone in *this* galaxy.'

They looked at each other, then glanced away. At that moment they measured their humanness against the same rule and were equal.

For they had turned at the same instant and looked outward

into intergalactic space, towards the infinitely remote light that was another island galaxy.

'It will be difficult to get there,' someone said.

They had lost a battle. There was no defeat.

UNTO MY MANIFOLD DOOMS

One by one I dismayed them, frightened them sore with my glooms
One by one I betrayed them unto my manifold dooms.

from *The Law of the Yukon*, ROBERT W. SERVICE

'Twelve, helmet lock,' Robson's voice rattled from the external speaker of his pressure suit.

'Twelve,' Sonny Greet echoed, glancing at the red arrows now point-to-point on the helmet and shoulder plate, then banging the closed latch with his fist. 'Aligned and locked.'

'Thirteen, bleed valve,' Robson read from the checklist mounted on the bulkhead.

'Thirteen, closed,' Sonny tapped the other man's suit with his knuckles.

'Fourteen, patch kit.'

'Fourtee...'

'What are you doing, Sonny, just what in the hell do you think you are doing?' Captain Hegg broke in, stomping across the airlock chamber towards them.

'Helping the prof with his checklist – I thought that was obvious, Cap'n.'

'Helping to kill him maybe. You are going to have to take this kind of thing more seriously. You didn't check that bleeder valve.'

'I looked at it, the handle is up and down like it always is. Closed – and I've never seen one of them open yet.'

'But you don't *know* until you have checked it,' Hegg insisted with slow patience. 'The handle might be broken, or turned a half turn.'

'But it's not, see Cap'n.' The tiny handle did not move when he pushed on it. 'So I was right all along.'

'You were not, Sonny. You did not follow checklist routine, that is all that matters.'

'*Mea culpa*,' Sonny insisted, raising his hands in mock surrender, grinning disarmingly. 'Have patience with my youth, Cap'n, and I promise never to do it again.'

'See that you don't.'

'You don't think I'm out to kill you, do you, Prof?' Sonny asked, looking ruefully away from the retreating back of the captain. 'If you were dead who could I possibly win a chess game from once in a while?'

'That's just Hegg's way, you know.' Robson's smile could just be made out through the thick viewplate of his helmet. 'He is really a good type, but terribly hardworking. He means well.'

'But why is it always my neck that gets caught in the bear trap when he is meaning well?'

Robson shrugged. 'We had better finish running through the checklist. I want to get those sample traps in before dark.'

'Right you are, Prof. We'll pick it up from fourteen.'

Sonny watched through their single-view port as Captain Hegg and Robson, slow and clumsy in their pressure suits, clambered over the nearby ridge and vanished from sight among the strangely earth-like trees. He shook his head, not for the first time, at the unreasonableness of it all.

'How about a game?' Arkady called from his bunk, holding up his pocket chess set. 'I'll spot you a rook.'

'Why commit suicide? You even won that game when you had no queen.'

'Just your bad luck, Sonny. With a queen ahead you could even win against the great Botvinnik, may his memory be revered, if you would remember to just keep exchanging.'

'Yeah, but I keep forgetting. Look, Ivan Ivanovitch, look out there at a sunny day on Cassidy-2. Wind in the trees, grass growing, maybe just a teensy tinge of green to the air that isn't quite earth-like. Doesn't it make you want to shake off your clothes and go out and take a walk?'

'Makes you want to be dead in five seconds,' Arkady answered heavily, setting up a problem on the board. 'The air out there is rich with deadly poisons and a mixture of hydrogen and methane that would burn with a lovely flame in this room.

Or in your lungs. Even the stones would burn in our air. Look how wonderfully Reshevsky sank Euwe back in middle ages, 1947.'

'Aw, come on, you know what I'm talking about. I could give *you* lectures about the natural wonders of this world. Remember I'm the mineralogist here and you are just a thick-headed Russky mining engineer. . . .'

'I go back to salt mine in morning.'

'. . . I'm talking about romance, emotion, art. Look out there. A world as close as the thickness of this wall, yet more unattainable than Earth, which happens to be light-years away. Don't you feel it? Don't you want to go out there?'

'I go out there without my suit I'll be dead in five seconds.'

'You're an unimaginative clod. If you are the end product of the Glorious Revolution I say bring back the Czar.'

'Da. It's your turn to cook today.'

'How could I forget? I was awake all night worrying about what to make for dinner. Will caviar go with beef stroganoff? Is the vodka cold enough?'

'Dehydrations and coffee will be fine with me,' Arkady answered imperturbably, concentrating on the chess board. 'You just torture yourself.'

'I'm worried about young Greer,' Captain Hegg said, after carefully making sure that he was talking through his suit speaker and that his radio was turned off.

'Sonny is a good chap,' Robson answered, plodding along at his side. 'He's not as young as all that either. He has his doctorate, he's done some very original work. I've read some of his papers.'

'It's not his work that bothers me. If he couldn't do it Spatial Survey would never have sent him out on this job. If there are the right kind of mineral deposits here he will find them and Barabashev will find a way to get the stuff out. I don't know anything about that, but I do know my job, which is running this expedition and seeing that everyone stays alive. And Sonny Greer is too careless out here.'

'He has had field experience before.'

'On Earth,' Hegg snorted. 'Antarctic, jungles, deserts. Kid stuff. This is his first offplanet trip and he is not serious enough about it. You know what I mean, Professor?'

'Only too well – since this is my eighth survey. And I am much more supernumerary than you are, let us not forget. The only reason the higher powers include a food-consuming ecologist such as I on these junkets is to stress the scientific value of new-planet work and to get a bigger appropriation come budget time. I have developed a very relaxed attitude towards this sort of thing from being on these expeditions, yet always being a bit on the outside. Give the chap enough time and keep after him. He'll catch on. Don't you remember me on my first expedition? Tanarik-4?'

Hegg laughed. 'How could any of us forget it? It must have been a month before the smell washed off.'

'Then you see what I mean. Everyone is green as grass at the start. He'll come around.'

'I suppose you are right.'

'There's something in my trap – look! A serpentoid and I swear – it has six legs!'

Two of the other traps also contained samples of the local life forms, and it took some time for Robson to poison them and transfer them to the sealed carrying case. There was no possible way to bring living specimens back to earth, or even to keep them alive in the dome with the restricted means available. The animals would have to be dissected and preserved in sealed plastic.

It was sunset when they started the trek back with the heavy carrying case, and it was dark long before they had reached the dome. But the directional beam came in clearly and the light on top of the radio mast was visible while they were still two kilometres away. Air might have been a problem, they were both on their reserve tanks, but they had more than enough left for the remaining time. The outer door of the lock was open and Hegg pulled it shut behind them, spun the wheel to seal it, then began the atmosphere evacuation pumps. Robson turned on the cleansing showers to wash away all traces of the alien atmosphere and soil from their suits.

The shower roared briefly, then died to a weak trickle.

'The tank is empty,' Hegg said, looking at the indicator on its side. 'Who was supposed to refill it?'

'Sonny – I think,' Robson said hesitatingly. 'But I'm not really sure of the roster.'

'I'm sure,' Hegg said grimly. He spun to the intercom phone on the wall of the lock chamber and leaned on the bell button.

'What's up?' the tiny speaker buzzed. 'This station on call day and ni . . .'

'You did not fill the shower tank, Greer. It is on your duty roster for today.'

'You're right, Cap'n. Clean slipped my mind worrying about dinner and all. Soon as you get inside I'll get right on it.'

'Can you tell me how we are going to get back inside if we can't rinse?'

There was only silence for long seconds. Then, 'I'm sorry about that. Just an accident. Is there anything we can do?'

'You're damn right there is. Get the drill and chuck in a bit with a diameter smaller than the filling hose from the reserve cans. Shave down the end of the hose, then one of you stand by with the tank while the other one drills a hole. As soon as the drill is through jam in the end of the hose – and I mean *fast*. You'll have a positive pressure on your side, so you'll be all right. We're in our suits. Then let in the shower fluid. We'll wash under the hose.'

'It sounds dangerous, Captain. Isn't there anything else?'

'No. Do it that way, and do it now!'

'I'm surprised they didn't build the tank in there with a pipe so it could be filled from in here.'

'The principle is to have as few openings as possible in a sealed bulkhead – and we can discuss the shortcomings of the designers some other time. Get that drill NOW!'

Captain Hegg waited stolidly while the endless seconds dragged by, but Robson could not control his growing concern. He kept glancing at his oxygen reserve indicator, tapping it nervously. The needle was almost to the *empty* mark. He jumped, startled, when a sudden shrill whining came from the silicon bronze wall. The whining slowed to a steady grinding noise and the black nose of the drill bit burst through the metal. It was jerked out and the hiss of incoming air ended abruptly as the tip of the hose plugged the opening. Liquid gushed from it.

'Do a good job of washing – and don't bother to look at your oxygen dial,' Hegg said. 'There is an unmarked safety reserve in all these tanks. We have more than enough time to do a complete job here.'

They scrubbed quickly with the heavy brushes, taking turns to wash the inaccessible parts of each other's suits. Robson had a stifling sensation that he knew was wholly imaginary and had to fight back an urge to scream when Hegg methodically washed the sample boxes, tilting them on end to get at their bottoms. More minutes dragged by as he went over them both, then carefully over the floor, with the sniffer. He found two suspect spots near the drain and had Robson scrub them while he finished clearing the area.

'All clean,' Hegg said, straightening up. 'And atmosphere evacuation is complete. Start the air pump and I'll crack the door.'

Air hissed in, but even though the inner door was unlocked it stayed sealed, held in place by the difference in atmospheric pressure. Robson stood before it, clenching his sweat-damp fingers inside the armoured gloves, fighting to appear as calm as Captain Hegg at his side. The sound of incoming air stopped and the door opened before them. Robson fumbled at the latch to unseal his helmet. Hegg already had his off, placed carefully in the rack, before he stalked into the dome, straight to the white-faced Sonny Greer who stood against the far wall.

'Do you know what you did? Do you have any idea just what you did?'

The words surprised the captain, because that was not what he had meant to say at all. Nor had he intended violence, yet his fist was clenched and his arm drawn back. *Christ*, he thought to himself, *do I want to kill the kid*? Toughened by experience on a dozen high-gravity worlds, his fist in that metal gauntlet would break the man's jaw, maybe his neck. It took more effort to relax than he had thought possible and he had to rub at the cable-hard muscles in his neck to force away the tension.

'I said that I was sorry, Captain. I mean that—'

'Will you get this through your thick head? Being sorry won't help me if I'm dead. You have had expedition experience before – earthside experience. What happens in the bloody Gobi desert or wherever you worked, if you don't fill the shower?'

'I—'

'I'll tell you what happens. Nothing happens. Someone maybe stays dirty for a while but that is all. And what happens here if you forget to fill the shower? Two men can die, that is what can happen! Does the difference penetrate, mister bloody stupid schoolboy?'

Sonny Greer's face was red, then suddenly white with suppressed rage. Robson was watching from the doorway where he stood, his helmet in his hands.

'Easy on, Captain,' he said in a worried voice. 'There's no need for all of this.'

'No, the captain is right,' Sonny broke in, his voice shaking, whether from anger or other emotion was hard to tell. 'I deserved that. And I'd lose my temper myself if someone pulled a stunt like that on me.' Arkady watched but said nothing.

Captain Hegg turned his back and became involved in removing his pressure suit so that the others could not see his face. He felt that his lips were pulled back from his teeth like an animal ready to bite, and a small, cool part of his consciousness wondered at the unexpected ferocity of his reaction. Moving with unhurried precision, he forced himself to remove and stow the suit before he spoke. He was in control of himself again. Arkady was helping Robson with his armour in the lock chamber; they could hear what was being said but not interrupt.

'Listen, Greer. I have nothing personal against you, I hope you realize that.' His voice was normal.

'I know that Cap'n. You're rough but square.'

Hegg chose to ignore the hint of amusement in Sonny's tones.

'I'm glad you realize that, so you will understand that what I

88

am going to do has no personal prejudice but is done by the book and for the good of the expedition as a whole. Have you ever heard of a planetary inefficiency rating?'

'No.'

'I didn't think you had. It is not a secret, but at the same time it is also not talked about much. The rules are simple. Two strikes and you are out. Out of the expedition, out of Spatial Survey and out of a job. You have just had your first strike.'

'What do you mean . . . ?'

'I mean exactly what I say. When I send in the weekly report tomorrow I am going to give you a negative efficiency mark. This will go on your record. It is not good, but it is nothing to be ashamed of, a lot of men have had them. The importance of the rating is double – to drive home the importance of regulations to you and to be sure you do not endanger anyone else's life. If you make one more blunder I send for your replacement.'

'Have a heart, Cap'n, it wasn't all that bad! No one was hurt. I promise nothing like it will happen again. I'll try doubly hard if you don't report this.'

'You will try doubly hard because I *do* report it. If I had any brains I would have sent in the first report when you didn't check the bleed valve on Robson's suit. If I had done that this would be your second mark and you would be out – which is where you belong. I don't think you have it in you to be a good spacer.'

He turned and walked away, as far as he could in the limited confines of the dome. Sonny stared after him, chewing his lip.

'I am hungry,' Arkady said, walking across the dome and looking into the pot that was simmering slowly on the electric stove. 'The stew smells as good as ever. Anyone joining me?'

'A bowl for me, if you will, Arkady,' Robson said, trying with slight success to keep a natural tone into his voice.

'Your heroic treatment seems to have worked,' Robson said looking out of the port to see if Sonny and Arkady were returning yet. 'Over two weeks now and your problem child has been good as gold, serious as a clam and attentive to his duty.'

'Not as serious as that. He is starting with the jokes again.'
Captain Hegg stretched his long fingers, cramped from labouring the keys of the minityper as he wrote up his report. 'He must take things seriously, all the time.'

'I think that you are worrying without cause. You know that it is possible for a man to have a sense of humour and still to be serious about his work. Good lord, you never seem to complain about my jokes, except that you don't think them funny.'

'A very different thing, Professor. No matter how you are feeling you always do your work the same way, correctly and methodically.'

'Some people use the term "old-maidish" for that.'

'Perhaps on Earth, where there are very few critical mistakes to be made. Out here it is essential to survive. A man must have it naturally, as you do, or force himself to learn it. Some never learn it and find jobs on earth. I would sleep much better if our mineralogist were there with them.'

'Speak of the devil. They're on their way back now, lugging a great ruddy trunk between them. I hope you filled the shower tank.'

'Of course! It's on my roster—' He caught Robson's eye and forced himself to smile in return, though he did not consider this sort of joke to be in very good taste.

The shower thundered and roared on the other side of the bulkhead. Hegg eyed the patch where they had drilled the hole and made a mental note to change it in the morning; the continual pressure changes could not be doing the flexible material any good. He wished, not for the first time, that their weight allowance had allowed for some metal-working tools. The sound of the shower stopped and the inner lock opened; the two men burst into the dome cheering and swinging the heavy case between them.

'So pure they won't have to bother to refine it!' Arkady shouted.

'The mother lode, the bonanza, the richest strike in the known history of man – no, in the history of the galaxy!' Sonny struck a noble pose, one foot on the case, arms flung theatrically wide.

'I gather you have found a new deposit of ore,' Robson observed dryly.

'Did you check with the sniffer before you bled in the air?'

'Of course, Cap'n, old watchdog!' Sonny was so lost in enthusiasm that he had the temerity to slap the captain on one massive shoulder and never noticed the sudden narrowing of his eyes. 'As of this very moment you can chalk up this expedition as a howling success!'

'It will be three months before the ship is here to take us off. Plenty of work yet. . . .'

'Paperwork and tedium, Cap me lad! The purpose of this trip was to see if rich enough deposits of titanium, beryllium or sodium could be found in great enough concentration to justify the installation of robot mining equipment, since it is impossible to bring in enough oxygen for large-scale human operation.'

'We have found it,' Arkady broke in. 'Almost a mountain of ore! Chunks of pure metallic sodium. I can see the installation now – a pithead, a spaceport. The robot miners, conveyers, the hum of mighty machines!'

'Whenever you Russians get poetic it is always tractors or mighty machines,' Captain Hegg said, catching the spark of their enthusiasm. 'Now climb out of those suits. And if either of you are capable of it, I would enjoy having a written report that I can send off as soon as possible.'

For a few hours that night the precariousness of their thin-walled bubble of air on an alien world was forgotten, for this was an event to be celebrated. Their survey was a success, even more successful than had been hoped for. The planet of Cassidy-2 would reluctantly release its precious metals and it would be the members of the expedition who received the credit for this largesse.

Captain Hegg rooted in the bottom of the container of the dehydrated fish that they all loathed, and brought up four steaks that he had hidden there for a deserving occasion. Robson, as acting medical officer, contributed a container of brandy from the hospital stores. The alcohol only added to their elation; they did not really need it. This was a night that would long be remembered. They retired late, calling back and forth from their bunks in the darkness, laughing outrageously at the sudden onslaught of Robson's snores, then one by one falling off to sleep as well.

Captain Hegg awoke possessed by the premonition that something was very wrong. He shook his head, cursing the muffling effects of the brandy, trying to understand why he had woken up. The room was dark, except for the glow of telltale lights from the instrument panel, and even from his upper bunk he could see that they all were glowing green. It couldn't be that. A red warning when the board was on night command set off enough alarms to lift them right out of their beds. What else? He coughed and cleared his throat.

With sudden panic he inhaled deeply and broke into spasmodic coughing. Smoke! There could be no smoke here! Smoking was forbidden, while very few things in the dome were even combustible. . . .

The ore case with the samples!

'Roll out!' Hegg bellowed as he half jumped, half fell from the high bunk and dived for the light switch. As his hand hit it he saw the red hairline gleam between the lid and the body of the sealed case.

'Get up! Get up!'

He pulled Sonny halfway out of his high bunk and at the same instant kicked Arkady in the side. This was all the time he could spare. He was aware of Robson stumbling up behind him as he dived for the case.

'Robson! Open the door to the lock chamber.'

The ecologist was tugging at the wheel even before he had finished speaking, and Hegg put his shoulder to the case and pushed just as the side burst open with roaring flame. Clouds of white smoke poured out and intense glare bathed the full wall of the room. Hegg fell backward, coughing and retching painfully. Sonny jumped over him and threw a wad of blankets and bedding over the flame. The resistant material covered the flame and checked the smoke for an instant while he and Arkady pushed the case towards the lock chamber door, now standing open.

Flame burst through the coverings almost instantly but they were at the door. Molten metal was dribbling from the flaming case and, pushing wildly, Arkady slipped and put his knee full into a pool of it. He rolled free, without uttering a sound, and beat the flame from his pyjama legs with his bare hands. At the same moment Robson and Sonny gave a last concerted heave and the leaking case slid into the lock chamber. They pushed at the door.

'Evacuation . . . pump . . .' Hegg managed to say through his coughing, but Arkady had dragged himself there with one leg and the motor was already whining.

The smoke was thicker before the last burning gobbet of metal had been shovelled up and dropped into the largest of their sample boxes. This was lined with heavier metal; before it burned through they had the lid sealed shut and an atmosphere of inert helium pumped in. The metal held, and in the lock chamber the burning also stopped as the combustible atmosphere was removed. With each passing second the air cleared as the air circulators drew out and filtered away the smoke.

'What happened . . . ?' Arkady asked, still dazed by the suddenness of the emergency. Blood ran down his leg, yet neither he nor any of the others noticed it.

'One of the locks on the sample case wasn't closed all the way,' Robson said thickly. 'I saw it just as I pushed the thing through the door. Right hand lock, open a couple of notches. Enough to let a trickle of air in. . . .'

'Who sealed that case?' Hegg's voice hammered at them, his coughing forgotten, or under control.

'I did,' Arkady said. Then, grimly, 'But Sonny opened it again to put in a last piece of ore.'

As though their heads were controlled by the same silent command they turned to face Sonny.

'But I didn't . . . well, maybe, it was an accident . . .' he said, his face slack, still stunned by the suddenness of the emergency.

Robson was closest. 'You – you –' he said, but could not find the words. With his shining bald head and jowled cheeks he should have looked funny as he stood there, shaking with rage, but he did not. Almost of its own volition his open hand sprang out and slapped Sonny across the face. Sonny stumbled backwards, his fingers fumbling towards the livid red mark on his white cheek.

Arkady hopped forward. His hard fist swung with all of his weight, caught Sonny on the side of the neck, knocking him to the floor. The three men fell on the writhing body, pummelling and kicking it, mouthing inarticulate sounds.

Captain Hegg ground his heel deep into the prostrate man's side just once before he realized who he was and what he was doing. He reeled away, then turned back to shout to the other two men. They did not hear him and kept on grimly at what they were doing. Pulling at them did no good either so he had to stop Arkady with a paralysing judo blow and drag the little professor over to his bunk and hold him there until he stopped struggling.

'Let me have the key to the medical supplies,' he said, when he saw that Robson was finally listening.

No one ever discussed the affairs of that night, except for the needed mechanical details of cleaning up the damage. Sonny Greer lay for three days in his bunk, bandaged and silent, closing his eyes when anyone came near. Arkady's burns were bandaged and he hobbled around the dome doing the minor maintenance work that he was capable of. Captain Hegg broke into fits of exhausting coughing if he did anything strenuous. Prof. Robson, though unmarked physically, seemed to have shrunk and his skin hung loosely. The three men kept very much to themselves, and when they talked did so in low voices.

It would be thirteen weeks before the relief ship arrived.

On the fourth day Sonny Greer climbed out of his bunk. Except for his bruised face and the bandages he seemed fit for duty.

'Is there anything I can do?' he asked.

Arkady and Robson turned away when he spoke. Hegg forced himself to answer.

'Just one thing. Arkady can't get into a suit, so you will have to go out with me once to get some more samples. After that you will be relieved of duty. You will stay in or near your bunk. You will touch none of the controls or equipment. Your meals will be brought to you.'

After that no one talked to Sonny, even when they handed him his food. The tension in the small dome grew worse with every passing day and Hegg wondered how long it would be before something really snapped.

Sonny had stumbled once, on his way from his bunk to the toilet cubby, and accidentally leaned on the air control console. Arkady had hit him once, knocking him halfway across the room. Hegg had been putting off the trip for the samples, but he finally forced himself to schedule it. Perhaps getting the man away from the others for a while would help.

'We are going after the ore samples tomorrow,' he announced to the room in general. The silence that followed was deadly.

'Let me check out your suit for you, Captain,' Arkady finally said.

'I'll help him.' Robson climbed to his feet. 'With two checking there are no errors. It's better that way.'

Hegg let them go. It was that way all the time now, the three of them checking and counter-checking each other, almost living in panic with their awareness of the manifold dooms that the planet held in store for them. Captain Hegg did not know how this situation could remain static for three full months. When the two men emerged from the lock chamber, he realized that Sonny was looking at him.

'Can I check my suit, Captain?' he asked. Neither of the men had gone near Greer's suit. It was as though he didn't exist.

'Go ahead,' Hegg said, then followed him through the door and watched his every move. It was a compulsive action he could not have resisted if he had wanted to.

The morning was worse. Sonny was forced to fumble into his suit by himself since the men ignored him, while at the same time they insisted on going through Captain Hegg's checklist three times before they were satisfied. The inner door had actually closed before Hegg could force himself to go over to the man, to run through the checklist with him. To touch Sonny's suit seemed repellent.

'One,' Sonny said. 'Spare oxy tank full.'

'One,' Hegg repeated, and with an effort of will drove his

fingers to tap the hated metal. They went slowly down the list.

'Thirteen, bleed valve.'

'Thirteen, closed.' And Hegg's fingers went out and felt the closed valve . . . then spun it open a half turn.

'Wait! There, it's all right.'

He sealed the valve again with palsied hands.

What had possessed him, he thought, as they left the lock and trudged slowly towards the distant hills? Why had he done that? He had not willed it. He would not kill Sonny, though he knew the man would be better off dead, before he did something that killed them all.

It was that simple. Sonny Greer was a menace. No longer a friend, he was in league with the planet, joined in battle against them. That was why the other two men shunned him like a Jonah. He *was* a Jonah. Worse than a Jonah. He was linked with the omnipresent powers that sought to destroy them, and they must both feel, as he did, that Greer would be better off dead.

At that moment Sonny Greer let go of his end of the sample case, stumbled and fell.

Hegg looked on, stunned, as he writhed on the ground, clawing silently at his helmet. Sonny's suit speaker was cut off and only muffled sounds came through the thick armour. Hegg bent over him, uncomprehending, as the man's body arched like a bow and collapsed. Hegg rolled him over and looked through the faceplate at the dead, tortured face.

His instant sympathy was overwhelmed by a feeling of immense relief.

Sonny seemed to have been killed by poisoning from the atmosphere. But how could it have entered his suit? There could be no leaks in the armour. Hegg would swear to that; he had checked it thoroughly himself. Then he remembered his traitor fingers at the bleed valve and he quickly tried it. No, it was sealed.

Or was it? The handle was tight to the stop and vertical – but wasn't there too much thread showing? Hegg turned the limp body until the sun shone directly into the mouth of the valve.

It was jammed half open by a particle of metal. The air in the suit would be forced out by the greater internal pressure, and when the pressure dropped the outside atmosphere would leak in. Had leaked in; because Sonny Greer was completely and finally dead.

Again the wave of relaxation swept over the captain, and it carried with it a tiny, nagging question.

How had the metal lodged into the valve? By accident? A lucky accident that made it stick in exactly such a way that the valve handle would look shut and feel shut – even though it was open?

'Cause of death, accidental,' Captain Hegg said, louder than he had intended, as he climbed to his feet and cleaned the alien dust from his hands, then rubbed them on his legs to cleanse them again.

'It had to be an accident. I can't very well list you as suicide,' he said to the unmoving body. 'It really should be self-defence, or justified homicide or something. But I can't say that, can I, Sonny?'

Now that death had removed the threat, he could feel for the first time the compassion that had been buried by his urge for survival.

'I'm sorry, Sonny,' he whispered gently, and touched the lifeless shoulder. 'You just shouldn't have been out here. I wish for all our sakes we had found that out earlier.

'Mostly for your sake though,' he said, rising. Then in a firmer voice. 'I'd better get back to the dome, straighten this mess out. . . .'

Beginning the long process of forgetting.

THE PLIABLE ANIMAL

> Man is a pliable animal, a being who gets
> accustomed to everything.
> —FEODOR DOSTOIEVSKY

Commander Rissby was squat and square, planted solidly behind the desk as if he had been grown there. He gave an impression of strength and determination – which was true, and of slowness and stupidity – which was completely false. He looked particularly bovine at this moment, scratching his close-cropped grey hair with one thick finger and blinking slowly while he talked.

'If I knew what you were looking for, Honourable Sir Petion, maybe then I could be of more help . . . ?'

The thin albino sitting opposite snapped his answer, cutting through the tentative advance of the Commander's words. 'What I'm doing here is my business – not yours. You will help me and you won't ask questions. At the proper time you will be informed. Not before. In the meantime you will be able to assist me. First thing – can you get me into the palace without arousing any suspicion as to why I am here?'

The Honourable Sir Jorge Suvarov Petion didn't really enjoy throwing his weight around. But it had to be done. It was one of the uncomfortable things that occurred in his line of duty – like looking at violently battered corpses. With other men he acted differently. He spoke to Commander Rissby in this manner not from malice but from previous knowledge. It was the only way one could get along with the stolid, unimaginative men of Tacora. They made the most loyal soldiers the Empire had – if you took into consideration their grim fixation with status. Speaking as he had, Petion established his superiority of person as well as of rank. His relationship with the Commander and his soldiers would now be a good one.

Truthfully, Commander Rissby was not insulted by the reprimand. He had questioned the other's authority and now knew where they both stood. The white-haired man across from him was one of those who held the Empire together. It would be a pleasure to take orders from him. He wasn't one of those pink-eyed social parasites who grew fat off the work of others. At the appropriate moment Sir Jorge would tell his reasons for being here. Meanwhile, the Commander could be patient.

Commander Rissby wasn't mentioning it aloud, but he could make a good guess as to what Sir Petion was really after. The palace, that was the key. Turning his chair slightly he could see it, just above the barracks roof, perched on top of the hill. An unusual structure, completely covered with overlapping ceramic plates, all of them in soft pastel colours. Like a candy castle. As if one good kick would send it smashing into a thousand pieces.

'You will have no trouble getting into the palace, Honourable Sir,' the Commander said. 'Not after your name and rank are known to the royal family. Very few of the nobility ever visit an off-the-track planet like this, and there is always an official invitation. Would you like me to . . .?' He added the question carefully, more of a suggestion than an interrogation.

Sir Petion proved he was not vindictive by nodding at the idea. 'Later. Not right now. I want to do a little looking around first. I'll need your help, but we can't be too obvious about it. Until the proper time you are the only person who is to know that I am an investigator.'

'As you say, so shall I act.' The Commander repeated the ritual words with sincerity, standing first and clashing the heels of his boots together as Sir Petion left.

Kai was waiting halfway across the barracks square, short and ugly as a tree stump. Even the squat Tacora soldiers towered over him, the one and a half Earth gravities of their home world having had only a slight effect on their height. Kai thought that four gravities were normal, and ruthless genetic selection had compacted his people into almost solid lumps of bone and muscle. His strength was beyond imagining.

There was no hurry in Petion's step, and apparently no direction. The boredom and diletantism of the nobility was well known, and made a perfect cover for an investigator's operation. As he strolled near Kai he snapped his fingers loudly. The short man trundled over with deceptive speed.

'What did you find out?' Sir Petion asked without bothering to look down.

'Everything, but everything, Georgie,' Kai rumbled. 'I copied the entire file while the clerk was out.' Kai had worked with the Honourable Sir long before he had been called by that title. He enjoyed a friendship shared by very few others.

'You mean you know who did it?' Petion yawned as he said it. Their conversation couldn't be overheard, and they kept up the appearance of master and servant to anyone watching from a distance. Kai gave a quick bow that seemed to break him in half and growled his answer.

'I'm good, old buddy, but I'm not *that* good. We've only been on this lightweight planet a couple of hours. But I have a complete transcript of the file, notes, observations – the works. It's a first step.'

'Well let's take a second one,' Petion said, starting off. 'The palace gate will probably be as good a place to start as any.' Kai scuttled after him as he left.

A brief walk took them to the palace. The streets weren't crowded, and the native Andriadans had a very low interest quotient. They made way for the white-haired Earthman, but did it in an automatic manner, their long legs working like stilts.

'Beanpoles!' Kai muttered, offended by the exaggerated length of their legs and thin forms. Any one of them could have stepped over him without breaking stride.

Kai had his notes concealed in an Andriadan guide book. He apparently read from the book, nodding at the pink, scale-covered wall in front of them. 'This is the main gate, the one the car came out of. At exactly 2135 hours according to the guard's log. It turned down the street behind us.'

'And Prince Mello was alone in it?' Petion asked.

'The driver said he was, and so did the gate guard. One driver, one passenger.'

'All right. How far did they go?' He led the way down the street.

'Just as far as this corner here,' Kai said, seemingly pointing at a mobile of ceramic bells that hung from the building, tinkling in the wind. 'The Prince shouted *stop* and the driver hit the brakes. Before the car had completely stopped moving the Prince opened the right-hand door and jumped out, running down this passage.' They followed the route the unlucky Prince had taken a year earlier, Kai tracing the course with his notes.

'The Prince left no orders, nor did he return. After a few minutes the driver began to be worried. He followed the same way – as far as this little intersection – and found the Prince lying on the ground.'

'Dead from a stab wound in the heart, lying alone, soaked with his own blood,' Petion added. 'And no one saw him, or heard him or had the slightest idea what had happened.'

He turned in a slow circle, looking at the intersection. Mostly blank walls broken by a few doors. There was no one in sight. Two other streets led away from the small square.

There was a thin creak of unoiled ceramic and Petion turned quickly. One of the doors had opened and a tall Andriadan stood looking at them, blinking. His eyes met the Earthman's for a single instant. Then he stepped back and closed the door.

'I wonder if that door is locked?' Petion asked. Kai had missed none of the interchange. He moved swiftly up the two steps and leaned against the door. It groaned but did not move.

'A good lock,' Kai said. 'You want I should push against it a little?'

'Not now. It'll keep. The chances are it means nothing.'

They took a different route back to the Imperial compound, enjoying the warmth of the golden afternoon. Andriad's primary glowed with a yellow brilliancy in the sky, coaxing pastel reflections from the sheen of the ceramic buildings. The air, the background murmur of the city, everything combined to produce a feeling of peace that the two men found alien after the mechanized roar of the central worlds.

'Last place you would expect to find bloody murder,' Kai said.

'My very thought. But are these people as relaxed as they look? They're supposed to be, I know. Peaceful, law-abiding agrarians, leading lives of unparalleled sweetness and domesticity. All the time – or is there a hidden tendency towards violence?'

'Just like that nice little lady boarding-house keeper on Westerix-IV,' Kai reminisced. 'The one who killed seventy-four lodgers before we caught up with her. What a collection of luggage she had in that storeroom . . . !'

'Don't make the mistake of assuming similarity just because of superficial resemblance. Many planets – like Andriad here – were cut off from mainstream galactic culture for centuries. They developed trends, characteristics, personality quirks that we know nothing about. That we *have* to know about if we are working on a case.'

'How about some original research,' Kai asked. 'In here.' He jerked his thumb at an outdoor restaurant, with shaded tables around a gently splashing fountain. 'I'm dehydrated.'

The Andriad beer was chilled and excellent, served in cold ceramic mugs. Kai sat opposite Petion at the table – no need to keep up the master and servant pretence here where they were unknown – and drained his beer almost at a swallow. He banged for more and rumbled deep in his chest as the waiter shambled slowly to fetch it. Sipping slowly at the beer he looked around the garden.

'Have the place practically to ourselves,' he said. 'The kitchen must be open, I can smell it. Let's try the local food. That army chow we had for breakfast is still sitting in my stomach, unchanged and undigested.'

'Order if you like,' Petion said, looking through the carved wood screen at the slow traffic of the street outside. 'I doubt if you will like it, though. In case you didn't read all of the guide book, the Adriadons are strict vegetarians.'

'No steaks!' Kai groaned. 'If I wasn't starving I wouldn't consider touching their slop. Order up – I'm game if you are.'

Petion left the choice of food to the waiter, who brought them a large compartmented tray filled with oddly-shaped bowls. Their contents differed in flavour and texture, but had an overall sameness.

'Tasteless.' Kai snorted and shook a coating of dried herbs over everything. He ate quickly, cleaning a number of bowls, hoping that quantity might make up for quality. Petion ate slowly, savouring the variety of flavours.

'The different dishes have their own charm,' he said. 'But the flavours are very subtle, never anything strong or over-powering like onion or garlic. If you make an effort to appreciate it, it's not too bad.'

'It's terrible!' Kai said, pushing away the empty plates and belching. A plate of exotic fruits occupied his attention next.

It wasn't that the scream was particularly loud or terrifying. It was just unexpected and completely out of place. The peaceful murmur from the streets and the delicate music of the wind-stirred ceramic bells was rudely sliced into by the suddenness of the cry. Kai choked on a mouthful of fruit, his glass knife falling and shattering on the stone floor; an ugly little gun appeared in his hand. Petion did nothing, just sat absolutely still and observed.

Waiters and customers, moving with haste unusual for Andriadans, crowded to the screen facing the street. Outside there were suddenly more people, pressing back against the walls on both sides of the street. They were all looking expectantly, and a little fearfully, in the same direction.

'What's the occasion?' Kai asked. The gun was gone now but he was still alert. The scream sounded again, closer and louder, and it was obvious now that it had been made by an animal of some kind.

'We'll know in a moment,' Petion said. 'Here they come.'

Men pulled on ropes attached to the large wooden cage, others pushed on bars fixed to the sides. The cage moved slowly, lurching and scratching along on wooden runners – even though wheels were used on all of the other Andriadan vehicles. This was something special. Everything about the cage and the fixed, half-horrified attention of the crowd spelled out the importance of the event. It was only the animal in the cage that seemed very unimpressive for the stir it caused. A mottle-furred, long-toothed and clawed carnivore, about the size of a terrestrial lion. It paced the cage, looking in bewilderment at the crowd. Again it opened its mouth and roared piercingly. A ripple of motion passed across the tall Andriadans.

'What is that beast?' Petion asked the customer nearest to him.

'Sinnd . . .' the man said and shuddered.

'What are they going to do with it?'

This question was obviously the wrong one, because the man turned shocked eyes on the Earthman. When Petion returned his gaze the Andriadan blushed and murmured something and turned quickly away.

'Pay the bill,' Petion told Kai, 'and let's follow that cage. This is something that is definitely *not* mentioned in the guide books.' The Sinnd's cry, muffled now by distance, echoed in the empty street.

By the time they had caught up with it the cage had almost reached its destination, an open field just below the palace. The cage had been pulled onto a raised platform and men with ropes gathered around it. Getting close enough to watch was no problem, since the native Andriadans seemed torn between horrified attraction and repugnance. There were large gaps in the crowd that stirred and shifted in an unceasing Brownian movement. An empty space surrounded the platform. Petion and Kai stood in the first rank and watched the strange ceremony approach its climax.

A webwork of ropes now held the Sinnd immobile. It mewled in terror as a noose pulled its head up, stretching its neck to the utmost. Thin white cloth was now wrapped firmly round and round its neck. The entire affair seemed meaningless.

'Look!' Kai hissed. 'The man in the white nightshirt. Recognize him from the photographs?'

'The King,' Petion said. 'This is getting more interesting all the time.'

Nothing was said from the platform and the affair proceeded at breakneck speed. It was over in less than thirty seconds. The King looked only once at the crowd and lowered his chin. A rustle swept the field as the gathered thousands bowed in answer. The King turned and took the sword from an attendant. With a single quick thrust he plunged it into the white wrappings, severing the bound beast's throat.

A voiceless gasp swept the audience as they drew in their breaths, almost in unison. Struggling against its bindings, the

Sinnd burbled a last horrible cry, then slumped down. The King withdrew the sword and the white bindings turned a brilliant scarlet. Next to Petion a man bent over and vomited on the ground.

He wasn't the only one, the repugnance seemed universal. There were only a few women in the crowd, and all had apparently fainted at the moment of execution, as had a number of the men. Their friends were quickly carrying them off. The field cleared with suspicious speed, even the King and officials from the platform joined the exodus. Within a minute the two offworlders and the dead beast were alone.

'Well I'll be damned!' Kai exploded. 'It wasn't that bad. Why I've seen infinitely worse things than that. I can recall . . .'

'Save your sordid reminiscences,' Petion told him. 'I've heard them all. In addition to which – you are correct. It *wasn't* that bad, particularly with the bandage to cover the wound.' He walked over and looked pensively at the slain Sinnd, freed of life and bondage at last.

'What does it all mean?' Kai asked.

'We're going to have to find out. The whole thing seems meaningless now, but it was obviously of great importance to the locals. Let's get back to the base and talk to Rissby. He's been stationed here nine years, and should know what it's about.'

'So you've uncovered the local secret,' Commander Rissby said. 'It's hard to tell if they are ashamed or proud of it. Anyway they make no attempt to stop people from watching, though they do fight strongly against any kind of publicity or official attention. Our policy during ninety-six years of occupation has been simply hands off.'

'Is it a religious ceremony?' Petion asked.

'Might be, Honourable Sir. We had an anthropology team through here once, and they were getting interested until they were officially requested to leave. One of them told me that the ceremony has an historical necessity that developed into a public ritual of exorcism.'

'How?'

'I don't know how much you know of this planet's history,

Honourable Petion ... ?' He hesitated, afraid to presume too much.

'For Empress's sake, tell us man!' Kai snapped. 'If you think Sir Petion has the time to bone up on the history of every off-trail planet – you're completely wrong. He knows what I tell him because I handle the mechanics of these investigations and keep the records. All he has to do is solve the problem. We know next to nothing about this rock, we came here direct from the last job and never got back to the archives.'

'Then you'll forgive a short lecture,' Commander Rissby said placidly, still knowing where he stood in the chain of command. 'Early history is obscure, but it is obvious this planet passed through a simple agrarian economy after being settled. Almost stone age, at least as far as artifacts go, since Andriad has no heavy metals. If the Honourable Sir has deemed it necessary to make a study of anthropology he will know that one of the theories of the development of mankind on Earth, concerned man's using his long legs for running, to escape predators. This happened, in actuality, right here. With no real mountains or forests, Andriad is a perfect habitat for herbivores. You've seen the gigantic herds that still roam the grasslands. Of course, as part of the ecology, there were the carnivores. One species dominated almost completely, the Sinnd that you saw today.'

'Men are better carnivores,' Kai said. 'So they knocked the Sinnd over the head and ate the ruminants themselves?'

'Quite the contrary. They ran away along with the other animals.' Kai snorted in contempt, but the other two ignored him. 'They became pure vegetarians – as they still are today. This period of food gathering and flight must have lasted quite a number of years.'

'But not for ever,' Petion said, 'or this city wouldn't be here. Sooner or later they had to stop running and find another way to deal with the carnivores.'

'Of course. They found that the Sinnd could be trapped in pits, captured alive. By this time they had developed such an aversion to taking life that they found it hard to kill. Rather they found it impossible. Yet a crime even worse than killing would be to let the animals starve to death. That was when

Grom – ancestor of the present King – started the royal family. He killed a trapped Sinnd. That's the way the myths have it and for a change they're probably true. Of course the rest of the Andriadans were horrified that a man could do this – yet at the same time strangely attracted. Grom was obviously the strongest man and quickly gained the power passed on to the present King Grom. They have all had the same name.'

'And the same job,' Petion said. 'Killing Sinnd. Does it happen often now?'

'Only a few times a year when a Sinnd will raid one of the towns. Most of them stay away, following the herds. Then the captured Sinnd is sent here to be despatched in the proper manner. The professor who told me all this also claimed it was a ritual murder of evil. The king-protector destroys the symbolic and the real devil at the same time.'

'Probably true,' Petion considered. 'It certainly explains what we saw today. Don't think these questions foolish, Commander. Everything on this planet is relevant to the case under investigation. I imagine you know why I'm here?'

'One can only guess . . .' Commander Rissby murmured politely.

'The murder of Prince Mello.'

'The murder of course,' Rissby agreed with no surprise.

'Tell me about Prince Mello. What kind of reception did he have here?'

Commander Rissby was no longer at ease. He mumbled something and suddenly his collar was tight enough to need easing with his forefinger.

'Louder please, Commander,' Petion asked.

'Prince Mello . . . why the Prince was of course a nobleman, a gentleman. All admired him and praised him. . . .'

'Rubbish and nonsense!' Petion exploded, angry for the first time. 'This is an investigation, not an attempt to whitewash the already tarnished name of a wastrel and a dolt! Why do you think a prince of the House, eighty-second cousin of the Empress, should be pleasure jaunting an out-of-the-way spot like this? Because the departed Prince's intelligence just cleared the moron borderline and he had trouble signing his own name.

Through stupidity compounded by arrogance he caused more trouble for the Empire than an army of iiberationists.'

Rissby's face and neck were flushed bright red. He looked like a bomb ready to explode and Petion took pity on him. 'You know all this – or suspected it,' he said gently. 'You must realize if the Empire is to prosper – as we both want it to prosper – some of the evils of generations of inbreeding must be eliminated. Mello's death was more of a blessing than a tragedy. Just the manner of his going reflects ill on the Empire and must be investigated. You are too long in the service not to know these things. Now tell me about the Prince's activities here.'

Commander Rissby opened his mouth, but no words came out. Loyalty fought with honesty. Petion respected the combination – knowing how rare it was – and treated the old soldier gently.

'It is no crime to discuss the faults of members of the royal family, since there is no doubt of your loyalty. You may talk safely to me.' Petion put his hand to one eye and when he removed it the iris was brown, in striking contrast to the pink albinism of the other eye. Rissby gasped.

'It is an open secret,' Petion said, 'that a reward of great service merits admission to the royal family. The Empress was good enough to reward my police work with a knighthood. With it goes the honour of royal albinism. I have had the operations to change my colouring, the manipulating techniques even changed my genes so the trait is hereditary in me now. I have not had the time for the eye operation – it means months in bed – so wear these contact lenses instead. So you see I am half of one world, half of the other. You can talk to me, Commander. You can tell me about Prince Mello.'

Rissby recovered quickly, with a trained soldier's resiliency. 'I thank you for taking me into your confidence, Sir Petion. You will understand then that I attempt no rumour or slander when I tell you that Prince Mello was – unpopular here....'

'That's the strongest term you can use?'

'Perhaps – *detested* might be a better one. It hurts me to say it, but it was the truth. My own soldiers felt it and only strong discipline kept them in line. The Prince laughed at the native customs, paid no attention to the peoples' sensitivities, blundered in where he had no business, in general he, you might say . . .'

'Made an ass of himself?'

'Precisely. He was tolerated by the Andriadans because of his nobility and his relationships with the royal family here. He was with them quite often. He favoured King Grom's daughter, Princess Melina, and I understand the attraction was mutual. She was so upset by his death that she was confined to her bed for weeks. I visited her myself, in the name of the Empress. Shock. Crying. Very unhappy case.'

'Then everything was peaceful inside the castle?' Petion asked.

'I would say so. King Grom is very reserved, so there is no way of telling his feelings at any time. But if he did not encourage, he certainly did nothing to hinder the romance of the royal youths.'

'What about in the city,' Kai broke in. 'Mello make enemies there? Go to gambling joints? Have girls? Associate with toughs?'

'Never!' Rissby gasped, shocked in spite of himself. 'The Prince may have had his failings, but he was still nobility! He rarely ventured into the city, and certainly had no acquaintances there.'

'Yet he did see someone in the city,' Petion said. 'Someone he knew well enough to recognize from a moving car at night. Someone he rushed to meet, never considering it a risk. Someone who may have killed him. I'll need more information on the Prince's activities outside of the palace. He may have been visiting the city unknown to you. Have you any spies or paid informers? Reliable ones I can contact?'

'Intelligence Section can give you more detailed information on that, though I don't think you will need it. We have one operative who has been consistently reliable, the only one I might say. His loyalty is to money and we see that he is well paid. He will tell you anything you need to know. Only you must go to him, he is never seen near the military compound.'

'The name?'

'One-finger. He has an unusual deformity of one hand. He keeps a low-class inn and drinking parlour in the Old Town. I will arrange for the proper clothes and someone to show you the way.'

No possible disguise could have made Kai resemble anything other than what he was. He grumbled at being left behind while Petion was slipping into the loose robes of a Turaccian trader. The Intelligence Officer, Captain Langrup, adjusted the outfit with professional skill.

'A number of traders come through here,' Langrup said, 'so two more wouldn't be noticed. A lot of them stay at One-finger's so this is a natural cover.'

'Do you have the caller?' Kai asked, taking the small, high-frequency receiver out of his pocket. Petion nodded and held up his hand with the ornate ring. When he pressed on the stone and twisted a shrill squeal blasted from the receiver. It warbled up and down when Kai changed the angle of the directional aerial.

'I doubt if we'll need to use it,' Petion said. 'We're just going there for information and there's no danger involved.'

'That's what you said on Cervi-III,' Kai scoffed, 'and you were four months in the hospital afterwards. I'll be hanging around close, ready to bust in.'

As Petion and the intelligence captain strolled through the Old Town they were barely aware of the stocky shadow that followed them. Kai was a good policeman, and a good tail even in the twisted labyrinth of dark passageways. Petion had lost his direction completely by the time Langrup turned into a black entranceway. It was a side entrance to a tap room. A noisy, badly lit place, filled with the stink of the burning weed the Andriadans smoked and the sweet pungency of beer slops. Langrup ordered two mugs of the best and Petion took careful note of the man who banged them down on the bar. His skin was sallow and wrinkled, the way it hung on the thin Andriadan bones it made him look like a walking skeleton. An accident or deformity had left him with only the index finger of his left hand. It appeared to be quite strong and he used it skilfully.

'We have some samples to show you,' Captain Langrup said. 'Shall we take them inside?'

One-finger only grunted, his eyes half-closed and flicking back and forth at both of them. 'Are the prices right?' he asked finally, the single finger scratching towards them across the bar, an animal nosing about for money.

'Don't worry,' Langrup said and pulled back the corner of his cloak so the full wallet could be seen hanging from his belt. One-finger grunted again and turned away.

'A repulsive type, but valuable,' Langrup said. 'Finish the beer then follow me.' They left by the main entrance, but instead of going all the way out into the street they climbed quietly up the stairs in the entranceway. There was a small room in the back of the building and they only waited a few minutes before the informer came in.

'Information costs money,' he said, and the finger scratched towards them again from across the table.

Langrup clinked ten of the translucent glass coins on the table. 'Tell us about Prince Mello,' he said. 'Did he ever come here to the city?'

'Many times. In his car. On the way to the palace or the country. . . .'

'Don't be devious!' Langrup snapped. 'We're paying for facts. Did he ever come *here*? Did he go anywhere else in the city? Did he have any friends here he visited . . . or girls?'

One-finger laughed, a crackling unpleasant sound. 'A girl! What girl could stand being near a Sinnd-smeller! He came here once and I had to fumigate the place afterwards. He told *me* that *my* place stank! He came here, went some other places, he never came back. There were no friends of his here . . .' his eyes half-closed again, '. . . or enemies.'

'What's this about being a "Sinnd-smeller"?' Petion asked the Captain. Langrup answered him, ignoring the informer's presence as though he were part of the furniture.

'It's a local idea, I'm not sure if it is true or just a way to insult us. They say that all off-worlders smell like Sinnd – that's a local carnivore. Say they can't stand to be near us too long. One-finger over there probably has plugs in his nose right now.'

'Is this true?' Petion asked him. One-finger didn't answer but grinned and tilted his head back instead, while the long finger leapt up and tapped at the white base of a plug barely seen in one nostril.

'Interesting,' Petion mused.

'Damned insult,' Langrup snapped. 'You're going to have to tell us more than that if you want your money,' he said to the informer. 'When I investigated a year ago you had no idea of who had killed Prince Mello. What do you know now? You've had plenty of time to hear rumours, find out things.'

One-finger was suffering. He writhed inside his skin and sweat stood out on his face. The questing finger ran out towards the money on the table, then retreated.

'You can get in bad trouble for withholding information,' Langrup said with angry intensity. 'Arrest, jail . . . even transportation. . . .' One-finger didn't even hear the threats, he was frightened enough already.

'Try money,' Petion suggested. 'I'll supply whatever funds are needed.'

Langrup slowly stacked high denomination coins on the table, and as the pile mounted One-finger began to shiver, pulling away. But his eyes never left the money.

'Here,' Langrup murmured, sliding the money slowly across the table, 'look at this. There's more here than you can make in a year of hard work. It's yours. Just tell us. . . .'

'I don't know who did it!' One-finger shouted hoarsely, falling forward across the coins, clutching them with his arms. 'I can't tell you that. I can tell you something. . . .' He gasped for breath and squeezed the words out. 'It was no one . . . from the city!'

'That's not enough!' Langrup shouted, standing and shaking the man so that the tempered glass coins sprayed down and rattled in all directions. One-finger's face was wide-eyed with fear, but he said no more.

'Leave him,' Petion said quietly. 'You're not going to get any more out of him. And he's told us what we want to know.' Not satisfied, Langrup slowly let go of the man, who dropped back into his chair as limply as if the bones had been dissolved from his body. They left him there and made their way back down the stairs.

'That's an awful lot to pay for so little,' Langrup said, not trying to disguise his dissatisfaction.

'It's enough,' Petion told him. 'It is really more than I expected to find out here. I would appreciate it if you would go back now and tell the Commander that I would like to meet with both of you, in his office, in about two hours time.'

'But I can't leave you alone here,' Captain Langrup said, shocked.

'I'm not alone as you see,' Petion told him. He had thumbed a message on his ring as soon as they had left the building, so he expected the squat figure that sidled up to them out of the darkness. Langrup gave a start. 'I assure you that Kai and I will be able to take care of ourselves,' Petion said.

'Can you find the square where the murder took place?' Petion asked after the intelligence officer had gone.

'With my eyes shut,' Kai scoffed, and led the way into an alley. 'What did you find out?'

'A little – or a lot. I don't know yet. The whole thing is still simmering in my head. There is just one more thing I would like to find out before reaching any conclusions.' They entered a square and he looked around. 'This is it, isn't it?'

'Crossroad of the Carved-up Corpse,' Kai agreed.

Petion looked around at the black doorways. He pointed. 'There's the one we saw open yesterday. I don't like to rely on coincidences, but they do occur. It also happens to be the one nearest the palace and we should look there first. Now's your chance to lean on it – but quietly.'

There was just enough light in the square to catch the white shine of Kai's grin. Climbing silently up to the door, he put one shoulder against it and his bar-like fingers clamped onto the carved stone jamb. A single contraction of his muscles pulled his weight forward a few centimetres. It was enough, a motion as sudden and powerful as a hydraulic ram. Something snapped sharply and the door swung open. They moved in quickly and closed it behind them. The building was silent.

'We're looking for a door,' Petion said. 'It may be in the wall or it may be in the floor. It will be concealed. I'll work this side and you work the other.'

Their lights threw wandering circles of radiance as they

searched. Only a few minutes passed before Kai called softly. 'Nothing to it. A real amateur job.' His light outlined a flag in the stone floor. The gap between it and the other stones was narrow and deep, clear of dust.

It took even less time to find out how it opened. When the stone slid aside they shone their lights into the black opening. A tunnel vanished into the darkness.

'If I were to ask you to make a guess – where would you think that tunnel goes?' Petion asked.

Kai bent down, and squinted along the length of the tunnel as far as his light could carry. "If it turns it could go anywhere. But if it goes on the way it starts it should end up bang in the centre of the royal palace.'

'That's what I would say myself,' Petion murmured.

'I should have made it clear earlier,' Petion told them. 'I want no notes or records kept of this meeting or anything else to do with this investigation. The Empress will have my report – and that will be the only one.'

'Sorry,' Captain Langrup said, and turned the recorder off and returned it to his pocket. Commander Rissby looked on quietly without commenting. All of their eyes followed Petion as he paced back and forth the length of the room.

'Some very important facts have come to light,' he said. 'One of the most interesting was supplied tonight by the informer. If he wasn't lying he has nàrrowed down our search for us. Whoever killed Prince Mello must have been from one of four groups.' He counted them off on his fingers. 'First – an Andriadan from the city or the country. Since the Prince had no contact with any of them, he certainly wouldn't have recognized someone and stopped the car. Group two are offworlders.'

'You can rule them out too,' Captain Langrup said. 'I worked on the original investigation. Every offworlder was grilled and cross-examined in detail. None of them could have possibly been the killer.'

'Then the third group is the military here. . . .'

'Sir!' Commander Rissby gasped in a shocked voice. 'You can't be suggesting . . .'

'I'm not, Commander – so set your mind at ease. Your Tacora troops might be suspected of a lot of crimes, but killing a member of the royal house is too unthinkable. In addition, I imagine the whereabouts of all your men were checked at the time?'

'They were – and eliminated from all suspicion,' the Commander said, only slightly mollified.

Petion folded a fourth finger into his palm. 'Then logic leads us to the conclusion that the murder was committed by a member of the final group. Someone from within the palace.' He smiled at their shocked expressions. 'Before you tell me that is an impossibility, that no one left the palace before the Prince, I should inform you of a discovery we made tonight.'

'A tunnel,' Kai said. 'Looks like it runs from the palace to the place where Mello got carved.'

'That could be it,' Captain Langrup shouted, jumping to his feet with excitement. 'A difference of opinion, a fight in the palace – we know that Mello left early – and while he is leaving the killer goes ahead of him. Calls to him, entices him into the alley – and kills him!'

'A nice construction,' Petion agreed. 'But there are some obvious holes in it that I won't bother pointing out, Captain. It *might* have been that way, but I do not think it was. The truth is a little more complex. I'll need a little more evidence before I will be able to state exactly. Could I talk to the driver of the car, the man who last saw the Prince alive?'

The Commander looked unhappy. 'I'm afraid that will be impossible, Honourable Sir. He was rotated six months ago, shipped out with his troop when their term of duty was up.'

'It's not important,' Petion waved the thought aside. 'I was expecting only negative evidence from him anyway. There is one more fact missing, with that the picture will be clear. Tell me about Prince Mello's eating habits.'

Only a shocked silence followed his words. The two army officers gaped and Kai grinned widely. He had little enough idea where the conversation was going, but was more used to Petion's turn of mind than the others.

'Come, come – that's a plain enough question,' Petion frowned. 'Simply looking at the Prince's photo and his height-weight index will show that he was overweight. Fat, if you are not afraid of the right word. Did this have an uncorrected glandular source – or did he overeat?'

'He overate,' Captain Langrup said as calmly as he could, trying not to smile. 'If you want the truth this was about the only thing that endeared him to the troops. Tacorans enjoy their food, and they were always a little awed at the quantity the Prince could put away.'

'During meals or between meals?' Petion asked.

'Both. He didn't talk much but I rarely saw him when his jaws weren't working. There was almost a path worn from his quarters to the back door of the cookhouse. The head chef became a close friend of his.'

'Get the chef up here, he's the man I want to talk to.' Petion turned to the Commander. 'Could you arrange for me to be invited to the palace tomorrow?' he asked. 'I would like to go to dinner there, the same place and the same hour as the Prince's last meal.'

Commander Rissby nodded and reached for the phone.

'I feel like an idiot in this outfit!' Kai whispered fiercely in Petion's ear, from where he stood behind him at the table. Dressed in colourful servant's livery he looked like a garishly painted tree stump.

'If it's any relief, you look like one too,' Petion answered imperturbably. 'Now be quiet and keep your eyes open for trouble from *any* direction. As soon as we have finished eating I'm going to stir this crowd up and see what develops.'

The banquet board was a large U with the royal family at the base of the U. As guest of honour Petion sat between King Grom and Princess Melina. The Queen had died in childbirth and the young prince was still a child, too young to sit at the adults' table. Since by Andriad custom only women of the royal family attended state banquets, the princess was the only female present. She was an attractive enough girl and Petion wondered idly what she had seen in that idiot Mello. Alien attraction and prestige seemed the only answer.

Both King and Princess were still unknown quantities. Frozen by protocol they could only discuss unimportant things in abstract terms. If anything King Grom seemed a little wary and on his guard. Which was understandable. His last noble guest had been butchered soon after leaving this same table.

Petion ate of the numberless different dishes and found himself enjoying the food. If you didn't mind not having meat with your meal this was good eating indeed. Herbs and spices in great variety, even hot little peppers that had scorched his mouth. He wasn't surprised when he saw that the Princess had taken a large portion of the peppers and was eating them with pleasure. She also oversalted her food. This underlined something he had suspected when he first heard her nasal voice and noticed the way she breathed through her mouth. A final bit of evidence that pulled his entire bundle of conjecture into shape. He had no foolproof evidence yet – but the theory seemed watertight.

He knew now just how and why Prince Mello had died.

After the final course the Princess excused herself and left. Which was just as well. What was going to happen next would not be pretty.

'Your Majesty,' Petion said, pushing his plate away from him. 'I have dined with you and would like to feel that we are friends.' The King nodded gravely. 'So you will pardon me if I sound unfriendly. I do so because I only wish to uncover the truth. The truth that has lain concealed too long.'

He had not spoken loudly, yet suddenly the table was quiet. Conversation dead in an instant, as though the talk had just been used to fill the time waiting for this moment. The dozen or more noblemen at the table all had their eyes fixed intensely on the tall albino next to the King. Behind him Petion heard Kai's clothing rustle and knew that man and gun were ready for action.

'You are talking about Prince Mello's death,' the King said. Not a question, but a statement. His Majesty was no coward when it came to facing things.

'Exactly,' Petion said. 'I don't wish to presume upon your hospitality, but this blot upon the relations of our peoples must be cleared up. If you will hear me out I will tell you what happened on that evening a little over a year ago. When I am finished we will decide what must be done.' He shifted position and took a sip of the royal beer. No one else moved and every eye was fixed unblinkingly on him. Petion felt grateful for Kai waiting alertly behind him. He turned to the King.

"You'll pardon the indiscretion, your Majesty, but there is a rather personal question I would like to ask you. Is it true that your daughter suffers from a minor physical disability?"

'SIR!'

'The question is important, or I wouldn't ask it. Am I correct in saying that Princess Melina has little or no sense of smell. That this is the reason she could bear Prince Mello's presence, even enjoy being with him. . . .'

'Enough!' the King interrupted. 'You are insulting the memory of a dead man and my daughter as well!'

'There is no insult intended,' Petion said, letting a cold touch of steel slip into the formal tones of his voice. 'If we are discussing insults I might mention the fact that your Majesty has filter plugs in his nose to enable him to bear my presence at his table. That could be called an insult. . . .'

King Grom had the good grace to blush red and made no further interruptions when Petion continued.

'There should be neither shame nor blame attached to what is a simple physical fact. All meat-eating animals have a characteristically strong odour – particularly to non-meat eaters. To your people the men of other planets smell bad. That is a simple and undeniable fact. Princess Melina – lacking a refined sense of smell – was unaware of this difference. She befriended Prince Mello and enjoyed his presence. She even asked him to dine here and you all put up with his presence for her sake. Until that evening when he did . . . what he did. And was killed for the repulsiveness of his crime.'

Petion's final words hung in a shocked silence. The unsayable had been said, the unspeakable spoken. Then a chair grated back and a young noble jumped to his feet, white-faced. Kai appeared at Petion's shoulder, gun pointing.

'You will sit down,' Petion said, 'and you and everyone else will be quiet until I have spoken. We are on very delicate ground here and I do not wish any mistakes to be made. You will hear me out.' He stared intensely until the man dropped back into his chair, then went on. 'Prince Mello committed the crime and died for it. You all witnessed it and by law are equally guilty. That is why I am addressing you together like this. The Prince was killed and you conspired to remove his body and conceal your crime.'

Some of the men were not looking at him now, but staring wide-eyed into space. Re-living that night they had tried to conceal and forget. Petion's voice flowed on as smoothly as the voice of memory.

'You stopped the flow of blood, but he was dead. You fought between yourselves as to what to do, but in the end all were convinced that dishonourable as it was the crime must be concealed. The only other alternative would be the end of everything as you knew it. You thought your monarchy could not survive a blow like this. So you undressed the corpse and one of you put on the dead man's clothes. In the darkness of the courtyard it was easy for him to get into the official car without being seen clearly. The driver said that no order was given, nor would one be necessary. There was only one place for him to drive to. The disguised man simply sat in the car until it passed the agreed-on spot, then shouted *stop* and leapt out. He ran to the square where his friends were waiting with the body, having brought it there through the underground passage. There was more than enough time to redress the corpse before the driver became suspicious. The deed was done. Mello had left the palace safely, and been killed by person or persons unknown. A tragedy, of course, but not a world-destroying one.'

'It is true,' King Grom said, rising slowly to his feet. 'The truth has been concealed. . . .'

'You can protect me no more your Majesty!' a shrill, almost screaming, voice cried. The same young man was on his feet again. 'I did it and I must pay the penalty, you have all protected me too long. . . .'

'KAI! STOP HIM!' Petion shouted.

With unbelievable speed the stocky body hurtled the table, crashing into the youth. But he was an instant too late. The man had his hand to his mouth, swallowing something. He didn't struggle when Kai pinioned his wrists.

'Majesty . . .' the man said and smiled. Then a shudder tore through his body, his figure arched back in sudden torture. Kai released his hands and the dead man fell to the floor.

'That was unnecessary,' Petion shouted, turning on the King, his face twisted with anger. 'Horrible waste!'

'I didn't know . . .' King Grom mumbled, sunk in his chair, older now.

'We could have arranged something . . . not *this*! That's why I'm here.'

'I didn't know,' was all the King could say, his face buried in his hands.

Petion dropped into his chair, suddenly exhausted. 'Well then, that's the way it will have to be,' he said. 'This man killed Prince Mello, then committed suicide rather than be taken. A life for a life. The rest of you will receive a reprimand for concealing the fact, and there will be a two per cent rise in the Empire duties on your planet for the next ten years. Agreed?'

From the shelter of his hands the King could only dumbly nod his head.

Commander Rissby was only confused after he read the report and the evening's affair had been explained to him. Petion was tired to exhaustion but held his temper well.

'This killer – the young man,' Rissby said, 'I don't understand. Why didn't they just turn him over to us for trial?'

'For the simple reason that he didn't kill the Prince,' Petion said. 'The King did. He was the only possible one. The insult was done to his daughter, directly in front of him. They all hate the taking of life, and would never consider it, even in anger. But the King is a killer – a ritual murderer perhaps – but the animals he kills are just as dead after the ritual. He kills with a knife and Mello was killed with a knife. The King must have been wild with anger and didn't realize what he was doing until it was all over. I'm sure he wanted to surrender then, but they talked him out of it. It would have meant the end of the regency and probably the royal family. For the sake of his planet – not for his own sake – he allowed the crime to be concealed. When I appeared the nobles must have sensed something in the wind and arranged for a suicide. Drawn lots or some such without the King's knowledge. A life for a life and the Empire still safe. The poison is a quick-acting one they use for euthanasia.'

'Then the King . . . ?' Rissby asked.

'Is the murderer. And he is undoubtedly punishing himself every hour of the day much more than we could ever do. I'm telling you this so you won't start thinking after I have gone and figure it out for yourself. And send in a report. The King's culpability will *not* appear in my final report. If it did he would have to be arrested. As it stands now the balance is straight and everyone is happy. At least on paper. I'll tell the Empress the truth – off the record – just as I am telling you. I won't need to swear her to secrecy as I am swearing you now. Raise your hand and touch the scroll.'

'I so swear . . .' Commander Rissby repeated numbly, still shocked. He finally stirred to life and tapped the report. 'But this – the roast leg of beef Mello got from the kitchen, what was wrong with that?'

'Use your imagination, Commander,' Petion said with barely concealed disgust. 'He brought this joint of meat, still steaming hot in insulating foil, unwrapped it and dropped it in front of the Princess, right there on the table. He was so stupid he thought he was doing her a *favour*, letting her try some good food for a change.'

'Yes . . . I know *what* he did. But why should the King kill him for a harmless thing like that?'

'Harmless?' Petion sat back and laughed. 'These people are strict vegetarians with an absolute horror of our eating habits. Just try to put yourself in the King's position. Let's say that you invited a cannibal home for dinner – he's reformed, but still a cannibal. And he has never quite understood what all the fuss was about. So he does you a favour, trying to introduce you to a whole new world of enjoyable eating.

'He drops a nice hot, steaming, crackling human arm on the table in front of you right in the middle of the meal!

'What would *you* do, Commander?'

CAPTAIN
HONARIO HARPPLAYER, R.N.

Captain Honario Harpplayer was pacing the tiny quarterdeck of the H.M.S. *Redundant*, hands clasped behind his back, teeth clamped in impotent fury. Ahead of him the battered French fleet limped towards port, torn sails flapping and spars trailing overside in the water, splintered hulls agape where his broadsides had gone thundering through their fragile wooden sides.

'Send two hands for'ard, if you please, Mr. Shrub,' he said, 'and have them throw water on the mainsail. Wet sails will add an eighth of a knot to our speed and we may overtake these cowardly frogs yet.'

'B-but, sir,' the stolid first mate Shrub stammered, quailing before the thought of disagreeing with his beloved captain. 'If we take any more hands off the pumps we'll sink. We're holed in thirteen places below the waterline, and . . .'

'Damn your eyes, sir! I issued an order, not a request for a debate. Do as you were told.'

'Aye aye, sir,' Shrub mumbled, humbled, knuckling a tear from one moist spaniel eye.

Water splashed onto the sails and the *Redundant* instantly sank lower in the water. Harpplayer clasped his hands behind his back and hated himself for this display of unwarranted temper towards the faithful Shrub. Yet he had to keep up this pose of strict disciplinarian before the crew, the sweepings and dregs of a thousand waterfronts, just as he had to wear a girdle to keep up his own front and a truss to keep up his hernia. He had to keep up a good front because he was the captain of this ship, the smallest ship in the blockading fleet to bear a post captain, yet still an important part of the fleet that lay like a strangling noose around Europe, locking in the mad tyrant Napoleon whose dreams of conquest could never extend to England whilst these tiny wooden ships stood in the way.

'Give us a prayer, cap'n, to speed us on our way to 'eaven

cause we're sinkin'!' a voice called from the crowd of seamen at the pumps.

'I'll have that man's name, Mr Dogleg,' Harpplayer called to the midshipman, a mere child of seven or eight, who commanded the detail. 'No rum for him for a week.'

'Aye aye, sir,' piped Mr Dogleg, who was just learning to talk.

The ship was sinking, the fact was inescapable. Rats were running on deck, ignoring the cursing, stamping sailors, and hurling themselves into the sea. Ahead, the French fleet had reached the safety of the shore batteries on Cape Pietfieux and the gaping mouths of these guns were turned towards the *Redundant*, ready to spout fire and death when the fragile ship came within range.

'Be ready to drop sail, Mr Shrub,' Harpplayer said, then raised his voice so all the crew could hear. 'Those cowardly Frenchies have run away and cheated us of a million pounds in prize money.'

A growl went up from the crew who, next to a love for rum, loved the pounds, shillings and pence with which they could buy the rum. The growl was suddenly cut off in muffled howls of pain as the mainmast, weakened by the badly aimed French cannon, fell onto the mass of labouring men.

'No need to drop sail, Mr Shrub, the slaves of our friend Boney have done it for us,' Harpplayer said, forcing himself to make one of his rare jests so loved by the crew. He hated himself for the falseness of his feelings, ingratiating himself into the sympathies of these illiterate men by such means, but it was his duty to keep a taut ship. Besides, if he didn't make any jokes the men would hate him for the slave-driving, cold-blooded, chance-taking master that he was. They still hated him, of course, but they laughed while they did it.

They were laughing now as they cut away the tangle of rigging and dragged out the bodies to lay them in neat rows upon the deck. The ship sank lower in the water.

'Avast that body dragging,' he ordered, 'and man the pumps, or we'll have our dinners on the bottom of the sea.'

The men laughed a ragged laugh again and hurried to their tasks.

They were easy to please, and Harpplayer envied them their simple lives. Even with the heavy work, bad water and an occasional touch of the cat, their existence was better than his tortured life on the lonely pinnacle of command. The decisions were all his to make, and to a man of his morbid and paranoic nature this made life a living hell. His officers, who all hated him, were incompetents. Even Shrub, faithful, long-suffering Shrub, had his weakness: namely the fact that he had an I.Q. of about 60 which, combined with his low birth, meant he could never rise above the rank of rear-admiral.

While he considered the varied events of the day, Harpplayer began his compulsive pacing on the tiny quarterdeck, and its other occupants huddled against the starboard side where they wouldn't be in his way. Four paces in one direction, then three-and-a-half paces back with his knee bringing up with a shuddering crack against the port carronade. Yet Harpplayer did not feel this, his cardplayer's brain was whirling with thoughts, evaluating and weighing plans, rejecting those that held a modicum of sanity and only considering those that sounded too insane to be practical. No wonder he was called 'Sapsucker Harpy' throughout the fleet and held in awe as a man who could always pull victory from the jaws of defeat, and always at an immense cost in lives. But that was war. You gave your commands and good men died, and that was what the press gangs on shore were for. It had been a long and trying day, yet he still would not permit himself to relax. Tension and the agony of apprehension had seized him in the relentless grip of a Cerberus ever since soon after dawn that morning when the lookout had announced the discovery of sails on the horizon. There had been only ten of them, Frenchy ships of the line, and before the morning fog had cleared the vengeful form of the *Redundant* had been upon them, like a wolf among the sheep. Broadside after broadside had roared out from the precisely serviced English guns, ten balls for every one that popped out of the French cannon, manned by cowardly sweepings of the eighth and ninth classes of 1812, grey-bearded patriarchs and diapered infants who only wished they were back in the familial vineyards instead of here, fighting for the Tyrant, facing up to the wrath of the death-dealing cannon of their island enemy, the tiny country left to fight alone against the might of an entire continent. It had been a relentless stern chase, and only the succour of the French port had prevented the destruction of the entire squadron. As it was, four of them lay among the conger eels on the bottom of the ocean and the remaining six would need a complete refitting before they were fit to leave port and once more dare the retributive might of the ships that ringed their shores.

Harpplayer knew what he had to do.

'If you please, Mr Shrub, have the hose rigged. I feel it is time for a bath.'

A ragged cheer broke from the toiling sailors, since they knew what to expect. In the coldest northern waters or in the dead of winter Harpplayer insisted on this routine of the bath. The hoses were quickly attached to the labouring pumps and soon columns of ice water were jetting across the deck.

'In we go!' shouted Harpplayer, and stepped back well out of the way of any chance droplets, at the same time scratching with a long index finger at the skin of his side, unwashed since the previous summer. He smiled at the childish antics of Shrub and the other officers prancing nude in the water, and only signalled for the pumps to cease their work when all of the white skins had turned a nice cerulean.

There was a rumble, not unlike distant thunder yet sharper and louder, from the northern horizon. Harpplayer turned and for a long instant, saw a streak of fire painted against the dark clouds, before it died from the sky, leaving only an after-image in his eyes. He shook his head to clear it, and blinked rapidly a few times. For an instant there he could have sworn that the streak of light had come down, instead of going up, but that was manifestly impossible. Too many late nights playing boston with his officers, no wonder his eyesight was going.

'What was that, Captain?' Lieutenant Shrub asked, his words scarcely audible through the chattering of his teeth.

'A signal rocket -- or perhaps one of those new-fangled Congreve war rockets. There's trouble over there and we're going to find out just what it is. Send the hands to the braces, if you please, fill the main-tops'l and lay her on the starboard tack.'

'Can I put my pants on first?'

'No impertinence, sir, or I'll have you in irons!'

Shrub bellowed the orders through the speaking trumpet and all the hands laughed at his shaking naked legs. Yet in a few seconds the well-trained crew, who not six days before had been wenching and drinking ashore on civvy street, never dreaming that the wide-sweeping press gangs would round them up and send them to sea, leapt to the braces, hurled the broken spars and cordage overside, sealed the shot holes, buried the dead, drank their grog and still had enough energy left over for a few of their number to do a gay hornpipe. The ship heeled as she turned, water creamed under her bows and then she was on the new tack, reaching out from the shore, investigating this new occurrence, making her presence felt as the representative of the mightiest blockading fleet the world, at that time, had ever known.

'A ship ahead, sir,' the masthead lookout called. 'Two points off the starboard bow.'

'Beat to quarters,' Harpplayer ordered.

Through the heavy roll of the drum and the slap of the sailors' bare horny feet on the deck, the voice of the lookout could be barely heard.

'No sails nor spars, sir. She's about the size of our longboat.'

'Belay that last order. And when that lookout comes off duty I want him to recite five hundred times, a boat is something that's picked up and put on a ship.'

Pressed on by the freshing land breeze, the *Redundant* closed rapidly on the boat until it could be made out clearly from the deck.

'No masts, no spars, no sails – what makes it move?' Lieutenant Shrub asked with gape-mouthed puzzlement.

'There is no point in speculation in advance, Mr Shrub. This craft may be French or a neutral so I'll take no chances. Let us have the carronades loaded and run out. And I want the Marines in the futtock-shrouds, with their pieces on the half-cock, if you please. I want no one to fire until they receive my command, and I'll have anyone who does boiled in oil and served for breakfast.'

'You are the card, sir!'

126

'Am I? Remember the cox'n who got his orders mixed yesterday?'

'Very gamey, sir, if I say so,' Shrub said, picking a bit of gristle from between his teeth. 'I'll issue the orders, sir.'

The strange craft was like nothing Harpplayer had ever seen before. It advanced without visible motive power and he thought of hidden rowers with underwater oars, but they would have to be midgets to fit in the boat. It was decked all over and appeared to be covered with a glass hutment of some kind. All in all a strange device, and certainly not French. The unwilling slaves of the Octopus in Paris would never master the precise techniques to construct a diadem of the sea such as this. No, this was from some alien land, perhaps from beyond China or the mysterious islands of the east. There was a man seated in the craft and he touched a lever that rolled back the top window. He stood then and waved to them. A concerted gasp ran through the watchers, for every eye in the ship was fastened on this strange occurrence.

'What is this, Mr Shrub,' Harpplayer shouted. 'Are we at a fun fair or a Christmas pantomime? Discipline, sir!'

'B-but, sir,' the faithful Shrub stammered, suddenly at a loss for words. 'That man, sir – he's *green*!'

'I want none of your damn nonsense, sir,' Harpplayer snapped irritably, annoyed as he always was when people babbled about their imagined 'colours'. Paintings, and sunsets and such tripe. Nonsense. The world was made up of healthy shades of grey and that was that. Some fool of a Harley Street quack had once mentioned an imaginary malady which he termed 'colour blindness' but had desisted with his tomfoolery when Harpplayer had mentioned the choice of seconds.

'Green, pink or purple, I don't care what shade of grey the fellow is. Throw him a line and have him up here where we can hear his story.'

The line was dropped and after securing it to a ring on his boat the stranger touched a lever that closed the glass cabin once more, then climbed easily to the deck above.

'Green fur . . .' Shrub said, then clamped his mouth shut under Harpplayer's fierce glare.

'Enough of that, Mr Shrub. He's a foreigner and we will

treat him with respect, at least until we find out what class he is from. He is a bit hairy, I admit, but certain races in the north of the Nipponese Islands are that way, perhaps he comes from there. I bid you welcome, sir,' he said addressing the man. 'I am Captain Honario Harpplayer, commander of His Majesty's ship, *Redundant*.'

'*Kwl-kkle-wrrl-kl . . . !*'

'Not French,' Harpplayer muttered, 'nor Latin nor Greek I warrant. Perhaps one of those barbaric Baltic tongues, I'll try him on German. *Ich rate Ihnen, Reiseschecks mitzunehmen?* Or an Italian dialect? *E proibito; però qui si vendono cartoline ricordo.*'

The stranger responded by springing up and down excitedly, then pointing to the sun, making circular motions around his head, pointing to the clouds, making falling motions with his hands, and shrilly shouting: '*M'ku, m'ku!*'

'Feller's barmy,' the Marine officer said, 'and besides, he got too many fingers.'

'I can count to seven without your help,' Shrub told him angrily. 'I think he's trying to tell us it's going to rain.'

'He may be a meteorologist in his own land,' Harpplayer said safely, 'but here he is just another alien.'

The officers nodded agreement, and this motion seemed to excite the stranger for he sprang forward shouting his unintelligible gibberish. The alert Marine guard caught him in the back of the head with the butt of his Tower musket and the hairy man fell to the deck.

'Tried to attack you, Captain,' the Marine officer said. 'Shall we keel-haul him, sir?'

'No, poor chap is a long way from home, may be worried. We must allow for the language barrier. Just read him the Articles of War and impress him into the service. We're short of hands after that last encounter.'

'You are of a very forgiving nature, sir, and an example for us all. What shall we do with his ship?'

'I'll examine it. There may be some principle of operation here that would be of interest to Whitehall. Drop a ladder; I'll have a look myself.'

After some fumbling Harpplayer found the lever that moved

the glass cabin, and when it slid aside he dropped into the cockpit that it covered. A comfortable divan faced a board covered with a strange collection of handles, buttons and divers machines concealed beneath crystal covers. It was a perfect example of the decadence of the east, excessive decoration and ornamentation where a panel of good English oak would have done as well, and a simple pivoted bar to carry the instructions to the slaves that rowed the boat. Or perhaps there was an animal concealed behind the panel, he heard a deep roar when he touched a certain lever. This evidently signalled the galley slave – or animal – to begin his labours, since the little craft was now rushing through the water at a good pace. Spray was slapping into the cockpit so Harpplayer closed the cover, which was a good thing. Another button must have tilted a concealed rudder because the boat suddenly plunged its nose down and sank, the water rising up until it washed over the top of the glass. Luckily, the craft was stoutly made and did not leak, and another button caused the boat to surface again.

It was at that instant that Harpplayer had the idea. He sat as one paralysed, while his rapid thoughts ran through the possibilities. Yes, it might work – it *would* work! He smacked his fist into his open palm and only then realized that the tiny craft had turned while he had been thinking and was about to ram into the *Redundant*, whose rail was lined with frighten-eyed faces. With a skilful touch he signalled the animal (or slave) to stop and there was only the slightest bump as the vessels touched.

'Mr. Shrub,' he called.

'Sir?'

'I want a hammer, six nails, six kegs of gunpowder each with a two-minute fuse and a looped rope attached, and a dark lantern.'

'But, sir – what for?' For once the startled Shrub forgot himself enough to question his captain.

The plan had so cheered Harpplayer that he took no umbrage at this sudden familiarity. In fact he even smiled into his cuff, the expression hidden by the failing light.

'Why – six barrels because there are six ships,' he said with unaccustomed coyness. 'Now, carry on.'

The gunner and his mates quickly completed their task and the barrels were lowered in a sling. They completely filled the tiny cockpit, barely leaving room for Harpplayer to sit. In fact there was no room for the hammer and he had to hold it between his teeth.

'Mither Thrub,' he said indistinctly around the hammer, suddenly depressed as he realized that in a few moments he would be pitting his own frail body against the hordes of the usurper who cracked the whip over a continent of oppressed slaves. He quailed at his temerity at thus facing the Tyrant of Europe, then quailed before his own disgust at his frailty. The men must never know that he had these thoughts, that he was the weakest of them. 'Mr Shrub,' he called again, and there was no sound of his feelings in his voice. 'If I do not return by dawn you are in command of this ship and will make a full report. Goodbye. In triplicate, mind.'

'Oh, sir—' Shrub began, but his words were cut off as the glass cover sprang shut and the tiny craft hurled itself against all the power of a continent.

Afterwards Harpplayer was to laugh at his first weakness. Truly, the escapade was as simple as strolling down Fleet Street on a Sunday morning. The foreign ship sank beneath the surface and slipped past the batteries on Cape Pietfieux, that the English sailors called Cape Pitfix, and into the guarded waters of Cienfique. No guard noticed the slight rolling of the waters of the bay and no human eye saw the dim shape that surfaced next to the high wooden wall that was the hull of the French ship of the line. Two sharp blows of the hammer secured the first keg of gunpowder and a brief flash of light came from the dark lantern as the fuse was lit. Before the puzzled sentries on the deck above could reach the rail the mysterious visitor was gone and they could not see the tell-tale fuse sputtering away, concealed by the barrel of death that it crept slowly towards. Five times Harpplayer repeated this simple, yet deadly, activity, and as he was driving the last nail there was a muffled explosion from the first ship. Hutment closed, he made his way from the harbour, and behind him six ships, the pride of the Tyrant's navy, burnt in pillars of flame until all that was left was the charred hulls, settling to the ocean floor.

Captain Harpplayer opened the glass hutment when he was past the shore batteries, and looked back with satisfaction at the burning ships. He had done his duty and his small part towards ending this awful war that had devastated a continent and would, in the course of a few years, kill so many of the finest Frenchmen that the height of the entire French race would be reduced by an average of more than five inches. The last pyre died down and, feeling a twinge of regret, since they had been fine ships, though in fief to the Madman in Paris, he turned the bow of his craft towards the *Redundant*.

It was dawn when he reached the ship, and exhaustion tugged at him. He grabbed the ladder lowered for him and painfully climbed to the deck. The drums whirred and the sideboys saluted; the bos'uns' pipes trilled.

'Well done, sir, oh well done,' Shrub exclaimed, rushing forward to take his hand. 'We could see them burning from here.'

Behind them, in the water, there was a deep burbling, like the water running from the tub when the plug is pulled, and Harpplayer turned just in time to see the strange craft sinking into the sea and vanishing from sight.

'Damn silly of me,' he muttered. 'Forgot to close the hatch. Running quite a sea, must have washed in.'

His ruminations were sharply cut through by a sudden scream. He turned just in time to see the hairy stranger run to the rail and stare, horrified, at the vanishing craft. Then the man, obviously bereaved, screamed horribly and tore great handfuls of hair from his head, a relatively easy task since he had so much. Then, before anyone could think to stop him, he had mounted to the rail and plunged headfirst into the sea. He sank like a rock, and either could not swim, or did not want to; he seemed strangely attached to his craft, since he did not return to the surface.

'Poor chap,' Harpplayer said with the compassion of a sensitive man, 'to be alone, and so far from home. Perhaps he is happier dead.'

'Aye, perhaps,' the stolid Shrub muttered, 'but he had the makings of a good topman in him, sir. Could run right out on the spars he could, held on very well he did, what with those long toenails of his that bit right into the wood. Had another toe in his heel that helped him hold on.'

'I'll ask you not to discuss the deformities of the dead. We'll list him in the report as Lost Overboard. What was his name?'

'Wouldn't tell us, sir, but we carry him in the books as Mr Green.'

'Fair enough. Though foreign-born, he would be proud to know that he died bearing a good English name.' Then, curtly dismissing the faithful and stupid Shrub, Harpplayer resumed walking the quarterdeck, filled with the silent agony which was his and his alone, and would be until the guns of the Corsican Ogre were spiked for ever.

'Just look at that gun barrel – big enough to poke your finger into,' Aram Briggs said, and did just that. With an unconsciously lascivious motion he pushed the end of his grimy middle finger into the muzzle of the bulky hand gun and rotated it slowly. 'Throws a slug big enough to stop any animal dead, hydrostatic shock, or if you use explosive slugs it can blow down a tree, a wall.'

'I should think the recoil would break one's wrist the first time it was fired,' Dr DeWitt remarked with unconcealed animosity, peering nearsightedly at the gun as though it were a snake preparing to strike.

'Where have you been living, DeWitt – under a rock? Break nothing, the recoil on a gun this size would probably tear your whole hand right off if it wasn't damped. This is a 25 mm. recoilless. Instead of kicking back, the energy is what we call dissipated by going out slots. . . .'

'Please spare me the inaccurate description of the principle of recoilless firearms; I know all I care to know on the subject. I would suggest you strap in before we start the braking descent.'

'What's the matter doc, you getting nervous. That's not like you to snap like that.' Briggs' grin was more sadistic than sincere and DeWitt fought against the automatic feeling of distaste it produced in him.

'Sorry. Nerves I guess.' That grin again. 'But I cannot say I am used to this kind of mission nor pretend that landing on a planet full of hostiles is in any way attractive.'

'That's why I'm here, DeWitt, and you should be damned happy I am. You science boys get yourself into trouble so you have to call on somebody who isn't afraid of guns to come along and pull you out.' A buzzer sounded and a red light began an irritated blinking on the control board. 'You let Zarevski get himself all hung up and you can't get him out by yourselves. . . .'

'They're going to drop this ship in sixty seconds, that was the warning to strap in.' DeWitt had of course seated himself as soon as they had left the parent ship for the small space-to-planet rocket, and carefully secured his straps. Now he glanced nervously from the large drifting shape of Briggs back to the flashing light. Briggs moved slowly, ignoring the warning, and DeWitt clenched his fists.

'Has the landing course been set?' Briggs asked as he slowly settled the handgun into his holster and even more slowly pulled himself down into the chair. He was still tightening his belt when the rockets fired. The first decelerating blast kicked the air from their chests and stopped any conversation until they cut off again.

'Automatically programmed,' DeWitt gasped, painfully inhaling and waiting tremulously for the next blast. 'The computer will put us into the area over the village where they are holding Zarevski, but we will have to land the ship. I thought we would set down on a level spot near the river, you remember it from the maps, it's not too far from the village.'

'Crap. We land right in the middle of the town, they got that great damned square or football field there, whatever it is.'

'You can't do that!' DeWitt gasped, scarcely noticing a course-correction blast that pushed him into the resilient chair. 'The natives will be there, you'll kill them.'

'I doubt it. We'll come straight down with the hooter going, flashing the landing lights and hover a bit before the final drop, there won't be one of those creeps left within a kilometre when we finally touch down. Any stupid enough to stay will get cooked, and good riddance.'

'No – it's too dangerous.'

'Landing by the river is even worse. You want these things to think we're afraid of them or something? Land that far away and you'll never see Zarevski again. We land in the town!'

'You are not in control yet, Briggs. Not until we land. But perhaps you are right about the river. . . .'

'You know damn well I am!'

DeWitt went on, ignoring the interruption. 'I can think of other reasons why it won't do to be too far away. Yet your landing inside the city is just as bad. We can't guarantee that some of them won't be caught in the landing blast, and that must be avoided at all costs. I think, if you look there on your map, grid 17-L, you'll see an area that will make a good compromise. It borders on the village and seems to contain a crop of some kind. And none of the photographs show any natives in the field.'

'All right, good enough. If we can't cook them we'll cook their corn on the cob.' His laugh was so short and throaty it sounded like a belch of disgust. 'Either way we'll throw a fright into them and let them know just what the hell we think and just why the hell they can't get away with this.'

DeWitt nodded reluctantly. 'Yes, of course. You probably know best.' Briggs did know best, that was why he would run the operation on the ground, and he, Dr Price DeWitt, with the myopic eyes and slightly rounded shoulders of a man who was more at home in a laboratory than an alien jungle, would be the second in command. It was not an easy thing to take orders from a man like Briggs, but it had been the decision of the Board and he had concurred.

Sending two men was a calculated risk, with the odds carefully determined by computer to be well weighted in favour of success. The only other alternative was a small-scale invasion by the military with no guarantee that their objective would be obtained. There would be few, or no, losses among the ranks of the invaders, but a number of natives would be killed and Zarevski would probably be assassinated before they could reach him. If this wasn't argument enough, Spatial Survey was morally and constitutionally opposed to violence against alien races. They would risk the lives of two men, two armed men who would only fight in self defence, and that was all. Aram Briggs and Price DeWitt had been the two men chosen.

'What's it really like down there?' Briggs asked suddenly, and for the first time the rasp of automatic authority was missing from his voice.

'Cold, a kind of particularly damp and nasty autumn that goes on for ever.' DeWitt worked hard not to show any of his natural feelings of pleasure at the light deflation of his companion's arrogance. 'This planet is a cold one and the natives stay near the equator. I suppose they find it comfortable, but on the first expedition we never seemed to be able to get warm.'

'You speak their language?'

'Of course, that's why I'm coming, I'm sure they briefed you about that. We all learned it, it's simple enough. We had to if we wanted to work with the natives since they absolutely refused to learn a word of ours.'

'Why do you keep calling them natives,' Briggs asked with a sly smile, looking at DeWitt out of the corners of his eyes. 'They have a name don't they? The planet must have a name?'

'It has an identification number, D2-593-4. You know Spatial policy on assigning names.'

'But you must have had a nickname for the natives, you must have called them something . . . ?'

'Don't try to be coy, Briggs, it doesn't become you. You know perfectly well that a lot of the men called the natives "creeps", just as you well know I don't use the name myself.'

Briggs barked a short laugh. 'Sure, doc. Creeps. I promise not to use the word creeps in front of you – even if they are creeps.'

He laughed again, but DeWitt didn't respond, sunk in his own thoughts, wondering for the thousandth time if there was any possibility of this rescue plan succeeding. Zarevski had been refused permission to visit this planet, had come in spite of this and had done something to anger the natives and had been captured. In the days that had passed since he had sent his last radio message he might have been killed. In spite of this it had been decided that a rescue attempt would be made. DeWitt felt a natural jealousy at this, that a xenologist could become so important that he could break all the rules and still be valued for his genius. DeWitt's own career of over ten years in the Spatial Survey was unmarked by anything other than a slow rise in position and an annual increase in salary. Pulling the eccentric Zarevski out of this self-made trap would probably be the most important entry in his record – if it could be done. And that was up to Briggs, the specialist, the man with the right abilities. A strident buzzer burst through his thoughts.

'The alarm, we are over the target area. I'll take control of the ship and land it. . . .'

'And as soon as we touch down I'm in charge.'

'You're in charge.' It sounded very much like a sigh the way DeWitt said it and he wondered again if there could be any sense to this plan.

Though DeWitt was theoretically flying the ship, he did little more than point to a spot and tell the computer to land on it. It was the computer that monitored the approach, measuring the multiple forces involved, cancelling them precisely with blasts from the jets. Once the final descent began all DeWitt did was watch the ground below to be sure none of the natives would be caught by the landing. The instant they touched down safely and the roar of the engines died away Briggs was on his feet.

'Let's go, let's go,' he ordered in his strident voice. 'Grab that box of trade supplies and I'll show you how to get Zarevski away from the creeps.'

DeWitt made no comment nor did he show his feelings in any way. He simply put the strap of the heavy box over his shoulder and struggled the weight of it towards the airlock. While the lock was cycling them out he zipped up the front of his heated coverall and turned on the power. When the outer door cracked open a keening wind thrust a handful of brown and strangely shaped leaves into the compartment, bringing with it the pungent, alien smell of the planet. As soon as it had opened wide enough Briggs pushed through and jumped to the ground. He turned slowly in a complete circle, gun ready in his hand, before grunting with satisfaction and shoving it back into the holster.

'You can come down now, DeWitt. None of them in sight.'

He made no attempt to help the smaller man, only grinning with barely concealed contempt as DeWitt lowered the box by its strap, then jumped down clumsily after it.

'Now let's go get Zarevski,' Briggs said, and stamped away towards the village. DeWitt trailed after him.

Because he had twisted sideways to straighten the strap over his shoulder, DeWitt caught sight of the three natives a moment before Briggs did. They appeared suddenly from a stand of yew-like trees and stared at the new arrivals. Briggs, who was constantly turning his head to watch on all sides, saw them a moment later. He wheeled, dropped, drawing his gun at the same time, and when he was lying flat on the ground he pulled the trigger. Nothing happened. The natives dropped just then.

DeWitt didn't move, though he had to control a sudden shiver that trembled his body. From his belt hung a small metal box with control studs on its surface; it looked like a radio-intercom, but it wasn't. He had his finger pressed on one of the buttons, and he didn't let up until Briggs had stopped pulling the trigger and began to examine the gun with horrified eyes.

'It didn't go off.... But why?'

'Probably the cold. Contracted the parts,' DeWitt said, hurriedly glancing from the prone man to the natives who were slowly climbing to their feet. 'I'm sure it will be all right the next time you need it. And it was a good thing that you didn't shoot. They weren't attacking, or trying to get close to us, just looking.'

'They better not try any funny business with me,' Briggs said, climbing to his feet and holstering his gun, though keeping his hand on the butt. 'They're ugly ones, aren't they?'

By any human standards the aborigines of planet D2-593-4 could not have been called attractive. They resembled men only in rough outline of body, head, and paired arms and legs on a thin torso. Their skin appeared to be covered with hairy scales: fish-like brown scales the size of a man's hand whose lower edge shredded into a fringe of furlike substance. Either they were moulting, or the random nature of scale arrangement was natural, because here and there on the bodies of all of them patches of scales were missing and areas of raw-looking orange skin shone through. They wore no clothes, only strings supporting containers and crude weapons, and the scales continued irregularly over all parts of their bodies. Their heads were perhaps their most repulsive aspect, covered with slashed and wrinkled orange skin. Both men knew that quivering slashes covered olfactory and auditory organs, yet the resemblance to mortal knife wounds was still disconcerting. The tiny eyes peered malevolently from another transverse slit situated near the top of the skull. DeWitt had spent more than a terran year on this planet and still found the sight of them repellent.

'Tell them not to come any closer,' Briggs ordered. He seemed unperturbed by their appearance.

'*Stop where you are,*' DeWitt said in their language.

They stopped instantly and the one on the right, with the most weapons, hissed through a mouth slit. '*You speak our language.*'

DeWitt started to answer, then restrained himself. It was a statement, not a question, and he was under strict orders to volunteer nothing. He was to act as much like a translating machine as possible since this was Briggs' show. Before he could translate the opening remark, the native went on.

'*How is it that you speak our language? Does this other one talk too?*'

'What is it jabbering about?' Briggs demanded, and snorted in anger when DeWitt had translated. 'Just tell him that your job is translating and I got no time to waste on that kind of stuff, and tell them we want Zarevski.'

This was a test of theory, and DeWitt took a deep breath before he answered. He put an effort into attempting to translate as exactly as possible and was surprised when they took no umbrage at the insulting tone of the words, in fact even bobbed their heads from side to side slightly in the local gesture of agreement.

'*Where did you learn our language?*' The leader asked DeWitt, who translated the question for Briggs before he answered.

'*On this planet. I was here with the first expedition.*'

Briggs was laughing. 'I bet they didn't recognize you, probably think all humans look alike – bet they even think *we* are ugly!' The smile vanished as quickly as it had arrived. 'Stop the horsing around. We came for Zarevski and that's all we care about. Tell them that.'

DeWitt did, having difficulty only with 'horsing around' though he managed to get the meaning across.

'*Come with me,*' the leader said, turning and walking towards the village. His companions went with him, but Briggs put a restraining hand on DeWitt's shoulder.

'Let them get a bit ahead. I want to keep my eyes open for

any tricks. And we don't want to do just what he says or he'll think he can push us around. All right, we can go now.'

At a respectable distance, as though they just happened to be strolling in the same direction by coincidence, the two parties straggled into the village. None of the inhabitants were in sight, though smoke rose from holes at the peak of most of the angled wattle and daub houses. The sensation of unseen eyes watching from their deep interiors was intense.

'*In there*,' the alien called back over his shoulder, at the same time jerking his many-fingered hand at a building no different from all the others.

The aliens kept walking on, without looking back, and Briggs stopped, quizzically watching them go. Only when they were out of sight did he turn and suspiciously examine the indicated building. It was perhaps five metres tall at the ridgepole and slanted straight to the ground on both sides. Narrow slits of windows let a certain amount of light into it, and the flat front was pierced by a doorway the size and shape of an open coffin. It must have looked that way to DeWitt too, because his nose almost twitched with intensity as he examined the black opening.

'No way out of it,' Briggs finally said. 'We have to go in and that door is the only way. You go first and I'll keep my eyes open.'

The difference between the two men was proven then in the most obvious manner possible. DeWitt had some natural qualms about going through the door, but he forced them down, mumbled his memory through the various forms of greeting, and bent over to step inside. He had just thrust his head in through the doorway when Briggs grabbed him by the shoulder and threw him backwards onto the ground. He landed painfully on the end of his spine, the heavy box crashed into his leg, and looked up in amazement at the thick spear sticking in the ground and still vibrating with the force of impact. It had penetrated deep into the earth in the exact spot where he had been.

'Well, that shows one thing,' Briggs exulted, pulling the dazed DeWitt to his feet. 'We've found the right place. This job is going to be a lot shorter and easier than I thought.' With one heavy boot he kicked the spear out of his way, bent under the door and stalked into the building. DeWitt stumbled after him.

Blinking in the smoke-laden air they could dimly see a group of natives at the far end of the room. Without looking around Briggs stalked towards them. DeWitt followed, stopping just long enough to examine the mechanism fixed over the door. Enough light penetrated from the slit windows so that he could just make it out: a frame fixed to the wall that held a heavy wooden bow two metres long. A rope, running towards the group at the other end of the building, had released the simple trigger mechanism. No part of the trap was visible outside the door – yet Briggs had known about it.

'Get over here DeWitt,' the voice bellowed. 'I can't talk to these creeps without you! Come on!'

DeWitt hurried as fast as he could and dropped his heavy box in front of the five natives. Four of them stood in the background, hands on weapons, eyes that reflected the ruddy firelight gleamed malevolently from thinned slits. The fifth alien sat in front of them, on a box or platform of thick woven wood. A number of pendant weapons, bangles and oddly shaped containers, the local mark of high rank, were suspended from his body and limbs, and in both hands he balanced a long-bladed weapon resembling a short sword with a thin blade.

'*Who are you?*' the alien asked, and DeWitt translated.

'Tell him we want to know his name first,' Briggs said, clearing his throat noisily and spitting on the packed dirt floor.

After a short wait, during which his eyes never left Briggs, the seated alien said, '*B'deska.*'

'My name is Briggs and I'm here to get a man like me who is called Zarevski. And don't pull any more tricks like that thing at the door because you're allowed just one free shot with me and you've had it. Next time I kill somebody.'

'*You will eat with us.*'

'What the hell is he trying to pull, DeWitt? We can't eat the local grub.'

'You can if you want to, some of the xenologists did though I never had the nerve. There is nothing in it to cause anything

141

worse than a bad heartburn, though I'm told the taste is loath-some beyond imagining. It is also an important social custom, no business is ever transacted except over a meal.'

'Bring on the chow,' Briggs said resignedly. 'I only hope this Zarevski is worth it.'

One of the other aliens put down his weapons at a hissed word and went to a darkened corner of the building, bringing back a gourd with a wooden stopper and two cups of crudely fired clay. He placed the gourd on the ground and one of the cups before the visitor and the other in front of the seated chieftain. Briggs squatted on his haunches, and reaching out he took up both cups and raised them at arms' length.

'Great cups,' he said. 'Great workmanship. Tell him that. Tell him that these ugly pieces of mud are fine art and that I admire his taste.'

DeWitt translated this, and while he did Briggs put the cups down again. Even DeWitt noticed that he had changed cups, so that each of them had the other's. B'deska said nothing, but pulled the plug from the gourd and first filled his cup with dark liquid, then Briggs'.

'Oh God, that's horrible,' Briggs said, taking a small sip and shuddering. 'I hope the food is better.'

'It will be worse, but you only have to take a token mouthful or two.'

The same native who had brought the drink, now appeared with a large bowl brimming with a crumbled grey mixture whose very smell provoked nausea. B'deska tipped a handful of it into a suddenly gaping mouth slit, then pushed the bowl over to Briggs who scooped up as small a portion as was possible. DeWitt could see a tremor shake his back as he licked it from his fingers. No amount of coaxing by the alien could force him to take a second sample. B'deska waved the bowl away and two smaller bowls of food were brought. Briggs looked down at his on the floor before him and slowly rose to his feet.

'I warned you, B'deska,' he said.

Before DeWitt had finished translating this Briggs stamped on the bowl, crushing it, then ground the contents into the floor with his heel. The alien who had served the food was running towards the door and in sudden realization DeWitt grabbed for the control unit on his belt, but this time he was too slow. Before he could touch the radio control that would prevent Briggs' gun from firing, the gun went off with a booming roar and the alien fell, a gaping hole in his back.

Briggs reholstered the gun calmly and turned back to B'deska who had raised his sword so that the point rested on the box next to him, but who otherwise had not moved.

'Now that that's out of the way, tell him I'm willing to talk business. Tell him I want Zarevski.'

'*Why do you want the man Zarevski?*' B'deska asked, his manner as unmoved as Briggs'. The dead alien lay crumpled, bleeding slowly into the dirt, and they both ignored him.

'I want him because he is my slave and he is very expensive and he ran away. I want him back and I want to beat him.'

'I can't say that,' DeWitt protested. 'If they thought Zarevski was a slave they might kill him. . . .'

His words were broken off as Briggs reached out and lashed him across the back of the face with his hand. It staggered him, bringing tears of pain to his eyes.

'Do what I tell you, you idiot,' Briggs shouted. 'You were the one who told me they kept slaves, and if they think Zarevski is a slave that will give them a chance to get a good price for releasing him. Don't you know that they think you are a slave too?'

DeWitt had not realized it until that moment. He translated carefully. B'deska appeared to be thinking about this, though his eyes were on the box of trade goods all the time.

'*How much will you pay for him? He committed a bad crime and this will cost a lot.*'

'I'll pay a good price. Then I will take him and beat him, then bring him home and make him watch while I kill his son. Or maybe I will make him kill his son himself.'

B'deska bobbed his head in agreement when this was translated, and after that it was just a matter of bargaining. When the agreed number of brass rods and paste gems had been taken from the box B'deska climbed to his feet and left the room. The other aliens picked up the ransom payment and left after him. DeWitt gaped after them.

'But – where is Zarevski?'

'In the box of course – where else did you think he would be? If he was valuable enough for us to come and get him B'deska wasn't going to allow him out of sight, or someone else would have made a deal with us. Didn't you see the way he had that pigsticker ready to stab down into the box. One wrong move of ours and he would have put paid to Zarevski.'

'But wasn't your killing one of his men a wrong move?' DeWitt asked, tearing at the strings that sealed the box.

'Of course not. There was poison in that bowl, that was obvious. So I killed the slave just like I told him I would.'

The top came off and inside, gagged and trussed like a pig, was Zarevski. They cut away his bindings and rubbed the circulation back into his legs so that he could walk. DeWitt supported him with one arm and Briggs waved them towards the door.

'Go on first and I'll come behind with the box. I don't think there will be any trouble, but if there is any you know that I can take care of you – slaves!' He laughed uproariously, all by himself.

They stumbled slowly through the empty streets and Zarevski smiled back over his shoulder. A number of his teeth were missing and there were clotted cuts on his face, but he was alive.

'Thanks, Briggs. I heard the whole thing and couldn't say a word. You handled it perfectly. I made the mistake of trying to be friendly with these damn snakes, and you saw what happened to me. Someone I had talked to died, and they said I had killed him with the evil eye, then grabbed. I wish you had been with me.'

'That's okay, Zarevski, people make mistakes.' His tone of voice left no doubt that he was one who never did. 'Only you'd better not talk any more until we're away from here. They saw you talking to me so you know what I have to do.'

'Yes, of course.' Zarevski turned back, closing his eyes, wincing even before the blow landed. Briggs raised his foot and kicked him in the back, knocking him sprawling. He made no attempt to help when DeWitt once more dragged him to his feet.

Once they were near the ship Briggs walked up close to them.

'Not much more, then we'll all be out of this.'

'Are you in Spatial Survey?' Zarevski asked. 'I can't say I remember your name.'

'No, this is just a temporary job.'

'You should make it permanent! The way you handled those natives – we can use men like you. Wouldn't you want to do that?'

'Yes,' Briggs said, he was sweating in spite of the cold. 'It's not a bad idea. I could help you people.'

'I know you could. And there is plenty of room for advancement.'

'Shut up, Zarevski! That's an order,' DeWitt broke in.

Zarevski dismissed him with a look and turned back to Briggs who was kneading his hands together with excitement.

'I could use an assistant like you on expeditions. I have enough men in the labs for writing up reports, but no one for field work. . . .'

'Be quiet, Zarevski!'

'. . . no one who really knows his way around like you do.'

'And do I!' Briggs shouted and threw his head back, tearing his fingers down his face, scratching the soft flesh. 'I can do it. I can do it better than anyone you know, better than anyone in the whole world. You're all against me but I can do it better. . . .'

'*Briggs!*' DeWitt shouted, turning and grabbing the man by both arms. 'Listen to me Briggs! Sunset-now! Do you hear me . . . SUNSET-NOW!'

With a tremulous sigh the big man closed his eyes and let his arms drop. DeWitt tried to hold him up but his weight was too great and he slumped to the ground. Zarevski looked on, dumbfounded.

'Come on, help me. You did this to him so you had better help carry him into the ship before B'deska and the rest of the locals see what has happened and come out after our skins.'

'I don't understand,' Zarevski said, helping to carry the dead weight to the ship, looking worriedly over his shoulder as the outer lock ground open. 'What's the matter with him?'

'Nothing now – before we left I planted the posthypnotic command with a key word just in case of trouble. He's asleep, that's all. Now we'll take him back to the hospital and try and put him back together. Everything considered he held up very well, and I would have got him back to the ship if you hadn't started your damn recruiting speech. Glory of Spatial Survey my foot!'

'What are you talking about?' Zarevski snapped.

Behind them the heavy door closed with a satisfying sound and DeWitt whirled to face the man they had rescued, anger finally burning through his control.

'Just who do you think Briggs is – a professional hero out of some historical novel that Spatial went out and hired? He is a sick man, right out of the hospital, and I'm his doctor – which is the only reason I'm here. One of the staff had to go with him, and I was the youngest so I volunteered.'

'What do you mean hospital?' Zarevski asked with a last attempt to bluster. 'The man's not sick. . . .'

'Mentally sick – and on the way to being cured until this happened. I hate to think how long it will set him back. Not as sick as some, he has almost a classic case of *paranoia simplex*, which is why we could use him. His delusions of persecution relate to his actual perception of his surroundings. So he was right at home down there. If you had read all the reports instead of blundering in you would have found out that those aliens have a society where a condition very much resembling paranoia is the norm. They feel that everyone is against them – and they are right. Everyone is. No sane person could have been counted on to have the right reactions in such a society – we needed someone who suffered from the *same sickness*. The only thing I'm even remotely happy about in this whole mess is that it wasn't my decision to send Briggs down there. They decided that upstairs and I did the dirty work. I and Briggs.'

Zarevski looked down at the slack face of the man on the floor, breathing hard even though he was unconscious.

'I'm sorry . . . I didn't . . .'

'You couldn't know.' Dr DeWitt was rigid with anger as he felt the fast, erratic pulse of his patient. 'But there is one thing you did know. You weren't supposed to land on that planet – but you did anyway.'

'That's none of your business.'

'Yes it is, just for now. Just for these few minutes before we go back to the ship and before I go back to my ward and they forget about me, with maybe a small commendation on my record, and you go back to being the great Zarevski and they put your name in the headlines. I helped pull you out of there which gives me the right to tell you one thing. You're a grandstander Zarevski and I hate your guts. I . . . oh what the hell. . . .'

He turned away and Zarevski opened his mouth to say something, then changed his mind.

It was a short trip back to the waiting mother ship, and they didn't talk to each other because there was really nothing to say.

I ALWAYS DO WHAT TEDDY SAYS

The little boy lay sleeping, the artificial moonlight of the picture-picture window throwing a pale glow across his untroubled features. He had one arm clutched around his teddy bear, pulling the round face with its staring button eyes close to his. His father, and the tall man with the black beard, tiptoed silently across the nursery to the side of the bed.

'Slip it away,' the tall man said, 'then substitute the other.'

'No, he would wake up and cry,' Davy's father said. 'Let me take care of this, I know what to do.'

With gentle hands he laid another teddy bear down next to the boy, on the other side of his head, so that the sleeping-cherub face was framed by the wide-eared unsleeping masks of the toys. Then he carefully lifted the boy's arm from the original teddy and pulled it free. Though this disturbed Davy it did not wake him. He ground his teeth together and rolled over, clutching the substitute toy to his cheek, and within a few moments his quiet breathing was regular and deep again. The boy's father raised his forefinger to his lips and the other man nodded; they left the room without making a sound, closing the door noiselessly behind them.

'Now we begin,' Torrence said, reaching out to take the teddy bear. His lips were small and glistened redly in the midst of his dark beard. The teddy bear twisted in his grip and the black-button eyes rolled back and forth.

'Take me back to Davy,' it said in a thin and tiny voice.

'Let me have it,' the boy's father said. 'It knows me and won't complain.'

His name was Numen and, like Torrence, he was a Doctor of Government. Both DGs and both unemployed by the present government, in spite of their abilities and rank. In this they were similar, but physically they were opposite. Torrence was a bear, though a small one, a black bear with hair sprouting thickly on his knuckles, twisting out of his white cuffs and lining his ears. His beard was full and thick, rising high up on his cheekbones and dropping low on his chest.

Where Torrence was dark Numen was fair, where short he was tall, where thick, thin. A thin bow of a man, bent forward with a scholar's stoop and, though balding now, his hair was still curled and blonde and very like the golden ringlets of the boy asleep upstairs. Now he took the toy animal and led the way to the shielded room deep in the house where Eigg was waiting.

'Give it here – here!' Eigg snapped when they came in, and reached for the toy. Eigg was always like that, in a hurry, surly, square and solid with his stocky body pressed into a spotless, white, laboratory smock. But they needed him.

'You needn't,' Numen said, but Eigg had already pulled it from his grasp. 'It won't like it, I know. . . .'

'Let me go . . . let me go . . . !' the teddy bear said with a hopeless shrill.

'It is just a machine,' Eigg said coldly, putting it face down on the table and reaching for a scalpel. 'You are a grown man, you should be more logical, have your emotions under greater control. You are speaking with your childhood memories, seeing your own boyhood teddy who was your friend and companion. This is just a machine.' With a quick slash he opened the fabric over the seam seal and touched it: the plastic-fur back gaped open like a mouth.

'Let me go . . . let me go . . .' the teddy bear wailed and its stumpy arms and legs waved back and forth. Both of the onlookers went white.

'Must we . . . ?'

'Emotions. Control them,' Eigg said and probed with a screwdriver. There was a click and the toy went limp. He began to unscrew a plate in the mechanism.

Numen turned away and found that he had to touch a handkerchief to his face. Eigg was right. He was being emotional and this was just a machine. How did he dare get emotional over it considering what they had in mind?

'How long will it take?' He looked at his watch, it was a little past 2100.

'We have been over this before and discussing it again will

149

not change any of the factors.' Eigg's voice was distant as he removed the tiny plate and began to examine the machine's interior with a magnifying probe. 'I have experimented on the three stolen teddy tapes, carefully timing myself at every step. I do not count removal or restoral of the tape, this is just a few minutes for each. The tracking and altering of the tape in both instances took me under ten hours. My best time differed from my worst time by less than fifteen minutes, which is not significant. We can therefore safely say – ahh,' he was silent for a moment while he removed the capsule of the memory spools, '. . . we can safely say that this is a ten-hour operation.'

'That is too long. The boy is usually awake by seven, we must have the teddy back by then. He must never suspect that it has been away.'

'There is little risk, you can give him some excuse for the time. I will not rush and spoil the work. Now be silent.'

The two governmental specialists could only sit back and watch while Eigg inserted the capsule into the bulky machine he had secretly assembled in the room. This was not their specialty.

'Let me go . . .' the tiny voice said from the wall speaker, then was interrupted by a burst of static. 'Let me go . . . bzzzzt . . . no, no, Davy, daddy wouldn't like you to do that . . . fork in left, knife in right . . . bzzzt . . . if you do you'll have to wipe . . . good boy good boy good boy. . . .'

The voice squeaked and whispered and went on, while the hours on the clock went by one by one. Numen brought in coffee more than once and towards dawn Torrence fell asleep sitting up in the chair, only to wake with a guilty start. Of them all Eigg showed no strain nor fatigue, working the controls with fingers regular as a metronome. The reedy voice of the capsule shrilled thinly through the night like the memory of a ghost.

'It is done,' Eigg said, sealing the fabric with quick surgeon's stitches.

'Your fastest time ever,' Numen sighed with relief. He glanced at the nursery viewscreen that showed his son, still asleep, starkly clear in the harsh infra-red light. 'And the boy is still asleep. There will be no problem getting it back after all. But is the tape . . . ?'

'It is right, perfect, you heard that. You asked the questions and heard the answers. I have concealed all traces of the alteration and unless you know what to look for you would never find the changes. In every other way the memory and instructions are like all others. There has just been this single change made.'

'Pray God we never have to use it,' Numen said.

'I did not know that you were religious,' Eigg said, turning to look at him, his face expressionless. The magnifying loupe was still in his eye and it stared, five times the size of its fellow, a large and probing questioner.

'I'm not,' Numan said, flushing.

'We must get the teddy back,' Torrence broke in. 'The boy just stirred.'

Davy was a good boy and, when he grew older, a good student in school. Even after he began classes he kept teddy around and talked to him while he did his homework.

'How much is seven and five, teddy?'

The furry toy bear rolled its eyes and clapped stub paws. 'Davy knows . . . shouldn't ask teddy what Davy knows. . . .'

'Sure I know – I just wanted to see if you did. The answer is thirteen.'

'Davy . . . the answer is twelve . . . you better study harder Davy . . . that's what teddy says. . . .'

'Fooled you!' Davy laughed. 'Made you tell me the answer!' He was learning ways to get around the robot controls, permanently fixed to answer the questions of a smaller child. Teddies have the vocabulary and outlook of the very young because their job must be done during the formative years. Teddies teach diction and life history and morals and group adjustment and vocabulary and grammar and all the other things that enable men to live together as social animals. A teddy's job is done early in the most plastic stages of a child's life, and by the very nature of its task its conversation must be simple and limited. But effective. Teddies are eventually discarded as childish toys, but by then the job is complete.

By the time Davy became David and was eighteen years old, teddy had long since been retired behind a row of books on a high shelf. He was an old friend who had outgrown his useful days, but he was still a friend and certainly couldn't be discarded. Not that Davy ever thought of it that way. Teddy was just teddy and that was that. The nursery was now a study, his cot a bed and with his birthday past, David was packing because he was going away to the university. He was sealing his bag when the phone bleeped and he saw his father's tiny image on the screen.

'David . . .'

'What is it, father?'

'Would you mind coming down to the library now. There is something rather important . . .'

David squinted at the screen and noticed for the first time that his father's face had a pinched, sick look. His heart gave a quick jump.

'I'll be right down!'

Dr Eigg was there, arms crossed and sitting almost at attention. So was Torrence, his father's oldest friend, who, though no relation, David had always called Uncle Torrence. And his father, obviously ill at ease about something. David came in quietly, conscious of all their eyes upon him as he crossed the room and took a chair. He was very much like his father, with the same build and height, a relaxed, easy-to-know boy with very few problems in life.

'Is something wrong?' he asked.

'Not wrong, Davy,' his father said. He must be upset, David thought, he hasn't called me that in years. 'Or rather something *is* wrong, but with the state of the world, and has been for a long time.'

'Oh, the Panstentialists,' David said, and relaxed a little. He had been hearing about the evils of panstentialism as long as he could remember. It was just politics; he had been thinking something very personal was wrong.

'Yes, Davy. I imagine you know all about them now. When your mother and I separated I promised to raise you to the best of my ability and I think I have. But I'm a governor and all my friends work in government so I'm sure you have heard a lot of political talk in this house. You know our feelings and I think you share them.'

'I do – and I think I would have no matter where I grew up. Panstentialism is an oppressing philosophy and one that perpetuates itself in power.'

'Exactly. And one man, Barre, is at the heart of it. He stays in the seat of government and will not relinquish it and, with the rejuvenation treatments, will be there for a hundred years more.'

'Barre must go!' Eigg snapped. 'For twenty-three years now he has ruled and forbidden the continuation of my experiments. Young man, he has stopped my work for a longer time than you have been alive, do you realize that?'

David nodded, but did not comment. What little he had read about Dr Eigg's proposed researches into behavioural human embryology had repelled him and, secretly, he was in agreement with Barre's ban on the work. But Panstentialism was different, he was truly in agreement with his father. This do-nothing philosophy lay a heavy and dusty hand on the world of politics – as well as the world at large.

'I'm not speaking only for myself,' Numen said, his face white and strained, 'but for everyone in the world and in the system who is against Barre and his philosophies. I have not held a government position for over twenty years – nor has Torrence here – but I think he'll agree that this is a small thing. If this was a service to the people we would gladly suffer it. Or if our persecution was the only negative result of Barre's evil works I would do nothing to stop him.'

'I am in complete agreement,' Torrence nodded. 'The fate of two men is of no importance in comparison with the fate of us all. Nor is the fate of one man.'

'Exactly!' Numen sprang to his feet and began to pace agitatedly up and down the room. 'If that were not true, if it were not the heart of the problem, I would never consider being involved. There would *be* no problem if Barre suffered a heart attack and fell dead tomorrow.'

The three older men were all looking at David now, though he didn't know why, and he felt they were waiting for him to say something.

'Well, yes – I agree. A little embolism right now would be the best thing for the world that I can think of. Barre dead would be of far greater service to mankind than Barre alive has ever been.'

The silence lengthened, became embarrassing, and it was finally Eigg who broke it with his dry, mechanical tones.

'We are all then in agreement that Barre's death would be of immense benefit. In that case, David, you must also agree that it would be fine if he could be . . . killed. . . .'

'Not a bad idea,' David said, wondering where all this talk was going, 'though of course it's a physical impossibility. It must be centuries since the last . . . what's the word, "murder" took place. The developmental psychology work took care of that a long time ago. As the twig is bent and all that sort of thing. Wasn't that supposed to be the discovery that finally separated man from the lower orders, the proof that we could entertain the thought of killing and even discuss it, yet still be trained in our early childhood so that we would not be capable of the act? If you can believe the textbooks the human race has progressed immeasurably since the curse of killing has been removed. Look – do you mind if I ask just what this is all about. . . ?'

'Barre can be killed,' Eigg said in an almost inaudible voice. 'There is one man in the world who can kill him.'

'WHO?' David asked, and in some terrible way he knew the answer even before the words came from his father's trembling lips.

'You, David . . . you. . . .'

He sat, unmoving, and his thoughts went back through the years and a number of things that had been bothering him were now made clear. His attitudes that were so subtly different from his friends', and that time with the plane when one of the rotors had killed a squirrel. Little, puzzling things, and sometimes worrying ones that had kept him awake long after the rest of the house was asleep. It was true, he knew it without a shadow of a doubt, and wondered why he had never realized it before. But it was like a hideous statue buried in the ground beneath one's feet, it had always been there but had never been visible until he had dug down and reached it. But he could see it now with all the earth scraped from its vile face and all the lineaments of evil clearly revealed.

'You want me to kill Barre?' he asked.

'You're the only one who can . . . Davy . . . and it must be done. For all these years I have hoped against hope that it would not be necessary, that the . . . ability you have would not be used. But Barre lives. For all our sakes he must die.'

'There is one thing I don't understand,' David said, rising and looking out of the window at the familiar view of the trees and the distant, glass canopied highway. 'How was this change made? How could I miss the conditioning that is supposed to be a normal part of existence in this world?'

'It was your teddy bear,' Eigg explained. 'It is not publicized, but the reaction to killing is established at a very early age by the tapes in the machine that every child has. Later education is just reinforcement, valueless without the earlier indoctrination.'

'Then my teddy . . . ?'

'I altered its tapes, in just that one way, so this part of your education would be missed. Nothing else was changed.'

'It was enough, doctor.' There was a coldness to his voice that had never existed before. 'How is Barre supposed to be killed?'

'With this.' Eigg removed a package from the table drawer and carefully opened it. 'This is a primitive weapon removed from a museum. I have repaired it and charged it with the projectile devices that are called shells.' He held the sleek, ugly, black thing in his hand. 'It is fully automatic in operation. When this device – the trigger – is depressed, a chemical reaction propels a copper and lead weight named a bullet directly from the front orifice. The line of flight of the bullet is along an imaginary path extended from these two grooves on the top of the device. The bullet of course falls by gravity but in a minimum distance, say a metre, this fall is negligible.' He put it down suddenly on the table. 'It is called a gun.'

David reached over slowly and picked it up. How well it fitted into his hand, sitting with such precise balance. He raised it, sighing across the grooves, and pulled the trigger. It exploded with an immense roar and jumped in his hand. The bullet plunged into Eigg's chest just over his heart with such a great impact that the man and the chair he had been sitting in were hurled backwards to the floor. The bullet also tore a great hole in his flesh and Eigg's throat choked with blood and he died.

'David! What are you doing?' His father's voice cracked with uncomprehending horror.

David turned away from the thing on the floor, still apparently unmoved by what he had done.

'Don't you understand, father? Barre and his Panstentialists are a terrible burden on the world and many suffer and freedom is abridged and all the other things that are wrong, that we know should not be. But don't you see the difference? You yourself said that things will change after Barre's death. The world will move on. So how is his crime to be compared to the crime of bringing *this* back into existence?'

He shot his father quickly and efficiently before the older man could realize the import of his words and suffer with the knowledge of what was coming. Torrence screamed and ran to the door, fumbling with terrified fingers for the lock. David shot him too, but not very well since he was so far away, and the bullet lodged in his body and made him fall. David walked over and ignoring the screamings and bubbled words, took careful aim at the twisting head and blew out the man's brains.

Now the gun was heavy and he was very tired. The lift shaft took him up to his room and he had to stand on a chair to take teddy down from behind the books on the high shelf. The little furry animal sat in the middle of the large bed and rolled its eyes and wagged its stubby arms.

'Teddy,' he said, 'I'm going to pull up flowers from the flower-bed.'

'No Davy . . . pulling up flowers is naughty . . . don't pull up the flowers. . . .' The little voice squeaked and the arms waved.

'Teddy, I'm going to break a window.'

'No, Davy . . . breaking windows is naughty . . . don't break any windows. . . .'

'Teddy, I'm going to kill a man.'

Silence, just silence. Even the eyes and arms were still.

The roar of the gun broke the silence and blew a ruin of gears, wires and bent metal from the back of the destroyed teddy bear.

'Teddy . . . oh, teddy . . . you should have told me,' David said and dropped the gun and at last was crying.

Also by Harry Harrison in Sphere Books:

THE STAINLESS STEEL RAT

Meet Slippery Jim diGriz cosmic criminal, the smoothest, sneakiest con-man in the known Universe. He can take any bank in the Galaxy, con a captain out of his ship, start a war or stop one – whichever pays the most.
So when the law finally catches up with the Stainless Steel Rat, there is only one thing to do – make him a cop. And turn him loose on a villainous lady who is building herself a battleship.

0 7221 4431 8   65p

THE STAINLESS STEEL RAT'S REVENGE

It was totally impossible for Cliaand to wage interstellar war ... but the crazy little planet was winning, whatever the odds. And there wasn't much the peaceful galaxy could do ... except send Slippery Jim diGriz – the Stainless Steel Rat – to wage his own kind of guerrilla campaign against the grey men of Cliaand and their leader, the indomitable Kraj. But then the Rat was aided by a band of liberated Amazons and his own beloved, murderous Angelina ... and they had to swing the odds in his favour.

0 7221 4432 6   65p

THE STAINLESS STEEL RAT SAVES THE WORLD

Someone was tampering with time, altering the past to eliminate the present, fading people out of existence into a timeless limbo.

One of the victims was Angelina, the lovely, lethal wife of James Bolivar diGriz – better known as the Stainless Steel Rat. That put Slippery Jim on the trail of the villains, a trail that went back to 1984 and an ancient nation called the United States of America. The Stainless Steel Rat was determined to rescue his wife. And before he was through he'd thrown dozens of centuries through time in *both* directions.

But then he didn't have much choice: to save Angelina he had to save the world. Again.

0 7221 4411 3   50p